# The Terrible Resurrection

The true tale of the search for a body stolen from its grave in 1878. Before the quest is over, it will involve the boards of three medical colleges in two states, the discovery of a body-snatching ring, a British spy, and reach into the very heart of the political arena to touch a future President of the United States.

## Curt Dalton

*To Jim & Patty,*
*Hope you enjoy!*
*Hawthorn Hill*

## ALSO BY CURT DALTON

*Breweries of Dayton*
*Home Sweet Home Front*
*How Ohio Helped Invent the World*
*Through Flood, Through Fire*
*When Dayton Went to the Movies*

*Cover: Background photograph is of Gregor Nagele. The oval portrait is of Senator John Scott Harrison, who was the son of William Henry Harrison and the father of Benjamin Harrison, both Presidents of the United States.*

Curt Dalton, 2058 Ottello Avenue, Dayton, OH 45414
daytondalton@prodigy.net

Printed by:

**Pr•gressive**
**PRINT ON DEMAND**

Dayton, Ohio

Many Thanks:

to the Magazine staff of the
Cincinnati Public Library

and to the staff of the
Bently Historical Library, University of Michigan

It's the people behind the scenes
that make an author look good

# INTRODUCTION

I have a passion for researching historical facts, especially when it involves the Dayton and Cincinnati, Ohio area. Imagine my delight to find that in the latter part of the nineteenth-century Cincinnati was once the home of a gang of grave robbers who made a living selling stolen bodies to local medical colleges. A few hours of research and I would have the basis for a nice little magazine article... or so I thought.

The first trouble I ran into was that almost all the criminal records for Cincinnati were destroyed in a fire at the courthouse in 1884. Rioters, who were tired of a legal system that seemed to be letting criminals go free, deliberately set the fire. Among the criminals in jail at the time were two men who had killed an entire family and sold their bodies to a local medical college, claiming that the family had died during a railroad accident.

But that's another story.

Disappointed, I began researching the local newspapers for any accounts on body-snatching that they might contain. What I found was a gold mine of information.

One particular occurrence of grave robbing stood out from the others. That story became the book that you hold in your hands today.

To make the narrative flow more smoothly I eliminated as many footnotes as I could. The notes that are left help breath life into the people that are written about in these pages. Although the story may seem fantastic, everyone mentioned in it existed and each lived the part they play in this tale.

Quotes that are not footnoted may be found in Cincinnati, Ohio newspapers during the time period of May 30 - July 2, 1878.

Curt Dalton

# Chapter One

*"Oh, Father, I should so like to be a Resurrection-Man when I'm quite grown up."*
-<u>A Tale of Two Cities</u> by Charles Dickens

The inside of the grave was dark, but the sound of the shovel hitting wood was unmistakable. They had reached the coffin.

In a few short minutes the upper portion of the coffin had been exposed. As one man stood watch, the other began drilling with an augur. When he was finished, he took a second to look at his handiwork. The holes were closely spaced in a slightly curved row crossing the width of the coffin lid about two feet from the top. Signaling to his partner that he was done, he handed out the augur and was given back one end of a hemp rope. They listened for a moment, and then the man inside the open grave stomped down hard on the lid of the coffin. The wood gave way with a large cracking sound, breaking across the holes, and the upper portion of the lid fell into the coffin.

Working quickly now, the man ignored the stench of the body that had been dead for four days. Reaching inside the coffin with both arms he lifted the corpse's head and tied the rope about its neck.

Climbing out of the grave, he and his partner tugged the body into a sitting position, then pulled it out of its confines onto the cold ground. The man who had been standing watch drew a knife and cut away the body's clothing, then deftly threw the naked corpse over his shoulder and carried it to a waiting buggy. His companion tossed the clothes into the coffin and began shoveling the dirt back into the grave.

The body was placed into a canvas bag and the tools were hidden away; in less than an hour from when they had begun the two men were off to Cincinnati with the stolen body.

# Chapter Two

*"(John Scott Harrison's) home was open to all, and his many friends were received with open heart and open hand. He was generous and providing almost to weakness and in assisting a needy friend, became poor himself."*
-<u>Cincinnati Journal</u> May 27, 1878

Home.

The word came to mind while Benjamin Harrison watched his father's house recede in the distance as the funeral procession made its way to the church. Although Benjamin had been gone for many years, that house, this land, was home.

As a boy Benjamin had roamed the 400 acres that his

father, John Scott Harrison, called Point Farm. Situated just five miles from North Bend, the farm formed the extreme southwest tip of Ohio, the land bordered by the Ohio and Great Miami rivers.[1]

Although Benjamin had visited only a few weeks ago, it still seemed as if years had passed. He was due to give a speech at the Republican State Convention and he had barely begun to write it. The Convention was to be held at the Metropolitan Theatre in Indianapolis on June 5, only a week away. After Indiana Senator Oliver P. Morton's death in 1877, Republicans looked upon Benjamin as the heir to the party's leadership and had asked him to be the chairman and keynote speaker at the State Convention.[2]

He smiled. His father had always said that anyone who became involved in politics was a fool. John Scott, called Scott by his family, had disdained crowds and so had not followed in his father's political footsteps, except for two terms in Congress for the Whig Party.[3] Being the third son of William Henry Harrison, President of the United States, had given Scott a taste of what devoting your life to politics could involve.

Yet, though Benjamin and his father disagreed over politics, it had never really interfered with their love for one another. Even after Benjamin eventually moved away to Indianapolis, Indiana, the two of them had kept in touch with constant letters and occasional trips.

It was at his home in Indianapolis that Benjamin learned of his father's death. On Sunday, May 26, 1878 Benjamin and his family had just returned from church when a messenger brought the telegram. The news came as quite a shock to Benjamin, as he had traveled to Point Farm earlier that spring and had found his father in good health. And just recently he had received a letter from Scott, telling of a twelve mile trip he had made by horseback to visit the grave of Augustus Devin, a daughter's nephew by marriage, who had died of consumption on May 18.[1]

The telegrams that followed told Benjamin about his father's last days. Scott had not been feeling well for a week or so. He had complained several times of chest pains, but they had not been severe enough to interfere with his customary outdoor habits. The day before his death, Scott had seemed more cheerful than usual, and spent the day riding over his farm and supervising its general management.

That night Scott had spent a quiet evening at home with Benjamin's brother Carter and his family. Carter had been living at Point Farm for some time, helping take care of his seventy-four year old widowed father. After dinner Scott had gone upstairs to polish up a speech he was writing called 'The Lay Element of the Church' which he had planned to deliver to the Cleves Literary Society in the Town Hall the following Friday.[5] The lecture topic was one on which he often wrote; the powerful influence mothers have in their children's religious training.

At 7 a.m. the following morning Scott was found lying on the floor of his upstairs bedroom by his grandson who had gone up to call him for breakfast. He had passed away sometime during the night. A small bottle of peppermint, which had been in the dining room on Saturday evening, was found in Scott's bedroom near him. It was believed that he had suffered chest pains during the night and had taken some of the peppermint to help relieve the pain.

Funeral services for John Scott Harrison were held at the Presbyterian Church at Cleves, Ohio on May 29 at 10:30 a.m. The 'Little Church on the Hill' had been erected with the help of Scott's father and mother and held a special place in the hearts of the Harrison family.[6]

As the funeral procession neared the church Benjamin was gratified to see that hundred's of Scott's neighbors were present, and many social and political acquaintances from Cincinnati were there to honor him as well.

Eight pallbearers carried the handsome metallic casket with its heavy silver handles into the church. One of the gentlemen, S. S. Smith, had been a pallbearer 37 years previously at the funeral of President William Harrison. Another pallbearer, William S. Groesbeck, had defeated Scott in his run for re-election to Congress in 1856.[7]

The funeral service was given by Reverend Horace Bushnell, an old and attached friend of the deceased.[8] Because he was blind Reverend Bushnell made his scriptural quotations, (of which there were many,) from memory. He likened the deceased to the Prophet Elijah who, after many trials and vexations, approached the end of his life with calmness and cheerfully hailed his translation to a better life. Then Rev. Bushnell proudly held up a letter written by the deceased in 1848, in which he thanked the minister for having led him to Christianity. It was at that time that Scott became an elder of the church, a position he had held for almost thirty years.

"A good man has gone from amongst us," stated Bushnell at the end of his sermon, "but it is my hope that the life and example of Mr. Harrison will not be lost upon the community in which he had lived so long."

Scott was buried in Congress Green Cemetery on a hill in the Harrison plot.[9] He was laid to rest next to his wife, Elizabeth Irwin, and not far from where Scott's father, mother and sister lay in the family vault.[10]

As the mourners made their way to Scott's burial spot, they passed Augustus Devin's grave. Someone noticed that the grave seemed to have been disturbed. Though some thought rooting hogs had done the work, others were afraid that the body had been stolen.

This was not an irrational fear rising from grief; in 1878 grave robbery was a common occurrence. The city of Cincinnati was not far away, and the need for cadavers for demonstration and dissection for the medical and dental students in the city's colleges was great. Hardly a week seemed to go by without some item of body snatching appearing in the local newspapers.

After the funeral, Benjamin's brother John, and George Coleman Eaton, Jr., their nephew, decided to examine Devin's grave. They found that the body had indeed been removed. The coffin lid had been broken. The coffin lid just over the head and breast had been broken away, and the tidy row of small scallop edges that showed in the wood indicated the use of an auger. Augers were the tool of choice for grave-robbers for their relative noiselessness.

Fearful of just this sort of violation, the Harrison family had taken precautions with their father's body. Scott's grave was made eight feet long and very wide and deep. Thomas M. Linn, a local stonemason and plasterer, was hired to line the bottom of the grave with stone, and build cemented brick walls to surround the coffin.[11] Three flat stones, eight or more inches thick, were procured for a cover. After the casket had been deposited in the grave, these stones were lowered in place with great difficulty. The largest, which was claimed to weigh over a thousand pounds, was placed over the upper part of the casket and reached two-thirds of the way to the foot.[12] Two smaller stones were then laid cross-wise on the vault to complete the cover. These stones were then cemented together. The grave was allowed to remain open for several hours to give the cement an opportunity to become thoroughly dried, and a guard stood watch over it the entire time. After the grave had been covered, and the dirt smoothed over, small wooden pegs were carefully inserted into the dirt just below the surface so that if the grave were disturbed their absence would notify the watchful friends of the fact at once.

Benjamin paid $30 to Linn to watch over his father's

grave. He directed Linn to visit the grave every hour during the night for one week, and to repeat his visits at intervals for a time until the body would be decomposed enough to not be of any use to the medical fraternity. Carter Harrison, angry after discovering Devin's body to be missing, gave Linn explicit instructions on what to do if someone tried to rob his father's grave.

"Don't come to me in the morning and say that somebody tried to rob that grave, and that he did not succeed; that you frightened him away; that you shot at him. If you have any report of that kind to make, come and tell me that he tried and that I can find his body there, on the grave."

Benjamin took a train back to Indianapolis later that same day so that he could ready his Convention speech.

While the rest of the family returned to North Bend, John Harrison and George Eaton decided to go to Cincinnati to try and recover Augustus' body. They did not inform his widowed mother, in the hope that Devin could be found and returned to his grave without causing her any more grief.[13] That evening they caught a train to Cincinnati. The search for Augustus Devin's body had begun.

# Chapter Three

*"A MYSTERY - About three o'clock this morning a
sensation was created on Vine Street by a buggy being
driven into the alley north of the Grand Opera
House...The general impression was that a 'stiff' was
being smuggled into the Ohio Medical College."*
-Cincinnati Enquirer May 30, 1878

The next morning John Harrison and George Eaton
made their way to Judge Vincent Schwab's office to
obtain warrants that would allow them to search the local
medical colleges for Devin's body. They had arrived in
Cincinnati late the evening before and had called on
Judge Schwab that same night, but he convinced them to
wait until the colleges opened in the morning.

Judge Schwab introduced them to Constable Walter

Lacy. Lacy showed them an article that had appeared that morning in a local newspaper, the *Cincinnati Enquirer.* It stated that at 3 a.m. a buggy had passed through the alley at the rear of the Medical College of Ohio.[14] The buggy had stopped about halfway through the alley and something white was taken out. Several men had started into the alley to see what was going on, when the buggy drove out onto Race Street and hurried away. The general consensus was that yet another body had been delivered to the medical college.

Although the men didn't believe it was Devin's body, since it had probably been taken much earlier in the week, it was enough for them to decide to begin their search there. On the way they met Detective Thomas E. Snelbaker, from the Independent Detective Police Agency, who agreed to accompany them.[15]

The Medical College of Ohio was on the south side of Sixth Street, between Race and Vine streets. The college was situated in a well-known, dreary building. It was the most prominent college in Cincinnati at the time, and an object of interest to passers-by for years.[16]

When the men arrived, their entrance into the college was delayed because they could not find the janitor, Aquilla Q. Marshall. After they located him they asked him to let them into the college.

"Well, now," the janitor hesitantly replied, "I think that I'd want for the officers of the college to be present during any search.

"Fine," Snelbaker agreed, "Go off and find them, and be quick about it. We've wasted half the morning on you already."

After the janitor left, Snelbaker decided to shadow him. Marshall, instead of going immediately to notify the faculty, made his way upstairs to the top floor and began to walk down a hall towards a back room. Glancing back and discovering he was being watched, Marshall turned around and returned to the group, saying that he didn't believe the faculty would be needed after all.

The men began their search at about one o'clock. They anxiously walked through the long halls, peering in at every door, examining every suspicious box, barrel, and pile of lumber from cellar to garret. In the cellar they found a large 'chute', or passageway, leading from the door which opened into the alley as described in the newspaper. It connected with a vertical chute, or well, that ran from the cellar to the top of the building. This, Marshall explained, was used for receiving the bodies delivered by the resurrectionists, and for elevating them to the dissecting rooms above. The men carefully searched the chute and the great furnace in the cellar (used for the cremation of the flesh cut from the bones of the 'subjects') but they found no bodies. However, they did find an unusual shovel near the chute. The handle was in two pieces, and was made to fit together by screwing one half to the other, like a pool stick. And, although coffee sacks were usually used to transport the corpses, a sac found in the chute was apparently new and made of thick, yellow canvas. These were gathered up as evidence.

Farther into their search the men came upon a student protectively dressed in coarse overalls and a shirt and vigorously at work on a body. He was cheerfully chipping away on his subject, the upper portion of a black woman and little piles of putrefying flesh lay about him in disorder. Only a small section of the head and breast remained intact. The woman's face had been terribly disfigured.[17]

They then passed a young man at work on some arms and legs. Noticing the group of men watching him, he told Marshall that the intruders should be ejected from the college, and that he was willing to pitch in and help. The janitor did not agree, nor did the "intruders".

Horrified, and almost unnerved by what they had seen, the men made their way toward the upper story room where the janitor had seemingly been headed earlier. Entering the room they found a miscellaneous collection of boxes, bundles, papers and bones. Among this they also discovered equipment which led them to believe that this room was also used for dissecting bodies. In the far corner was a curious thing- a windlass, similar to the kind used to draw water from a well. The rope hung into a hole in the floor. At each side of the hole was a heavy beam, which supported the windlass. There was a trap door, which could be used to cover the hole when the windlass wasn't in use.

A search of the room uncovered no bodies. Disheartened, the men were about to give up when Snelbaker felt the rope. It was taut, as if a weight were on the other end.

"Here, somebody," he said, seizing the crank and turning the windlass. "Hold on, there may be something on this rope."

It was evident that something was indeed attached, as the turning required some effort on Snelbaker's part. During this time, Dr. William W. Seely, the executive officer of the college, entered the room.[18] After some ten minutes of vigorous hoisting a body emerged, completely naked except for a cloth, which covered its head and shoulders. The men realized that the janitor had meant to come up and cut the rope so that the body would fall down the chute and not be discovered.

"It is not the man for whom I am looking," said John, preparing to give up the search. "He died of consumption and was more emaciated than this one."

Eaton agreed. "That's an old man," he said, spying the gray hair that showed at the margin of the cloth that covered the body's face. "We're after a young man."

Snelbaker insisted they examine the body. "You had better look at the face." he said. "You might be mistaken and you'll never forgive yourself if you allow any doubtful point to trespass."

"It is hardly necessary," said John hesitantly, desiring to retreat. "Still, if you insist, I will do so."

The body was raised out of the well and the trap door shut beneath it. The rope had been rudely tied about the neck, and as the body was lowered, the head fell forward and what looked to be blood or embalming fluid streamed from an incision in the neck. Loosening the rope, the body fell to the floor, the light from the window directly overhead shone over the head and shoulders. Snelbaker reached down and removed the cloth.

The features of an old man were revealed, with a full white beard cut squarely off an inch below the chin. The face was discolored and white from the pressure of the rope and the rough handling it had received.

"It is definitely an old man," said Dr. Seely. "Since you have not found the body of the young man, it would do well not to say anything to the mother. If she is ignorant of the truth she will suffer no grief."

John was not listening. He had stooped down to take a parting look at the corpse, when suddenly the blood fled from his face, and he looked as white as the body at which he peered so closely.

"What is the matter?" asked Snelbaker, stepping quickly to him.

John remain silent, his eyes widening as he gazed upon the face of the dead man before him. Supporting himself upon the arm of the detective, he recovered enough to gasp, "It's my father!"

A hasty examination ensued to make sure that the body was truly that of Scott Harrison. The long, snowy beard, which had nearly reached to his waist, had been cut off and the face disfigured, but the body was recognizable. Scott had fallen when he died, and his face had received a slight skin bruise on the right side of the forehead. The bruise was there, as well as a mole on the forehead, which John recognized.

Dr. Seely didn't understand the fuss being made over

the body.

"Well, it will all be the same on the day of resurrection." he said.

Sobbing with grief and shock, John drew out a small tobacco knife from his pocket and sat down beside the corpse of his father.

"I'll guard him," he said to George, "while you run and get an undertaker."

Eaton left at once.

# Chapter Four

*"And let them watch over me for three weeks,*
*My wretched corpse to save,*
*For then I think that I may stink,*
*Enough to rest in my grave."*
-The Surgeon's Warning by Robert Southey

When Thomas Linn returned to Scott's grave in the morning, he noticed a difference between the head and the foot of the mound in the matter of the finish of the dirt. Linn told Archie Eaton, George's younger brother, of his suspicions.

Every precaution was taken to prevent the news from spreading. The men who were summoned to open the grave were directed to approach the cemetery at different times and from different directions so as not to arouse any excitement. The shovels were struck into the earth. Hardly two feet down they found one of the smaller stones which had formed the lid of the vault; they knew this was positive evidence that the grave had been disturbed. When they reached the vault they found that the two stones which had lain across the foot of the grave had been lifted on end, the casket broken into and the body drawn out feet first. The box containing the casket had been opened by making a curved row of augur holes in the pine wood, just as when Devin's body had been taken. The lid of the casket was then pried up with a strong tool, the glass seal broken, and the body drawn out.

Since the usual way for a resurrectionist to extract a body from a grave was to draw it out by the head, it was believed that whoever was responsible for Scott's disinterment had been present at the time of his burial and had noticed the smaller stones being placed at the foot of the coffin. Benjamin Harrison was positive this had occurred.

"When my wife stood by my side at the grave," he later stated to the press, "we noticed a man push by us in an obtrusive manner and peer into the grave with an unexpected amount of curiosity. This manner in which the robbers evidently began and completed their work leads me to conclude that they must have known every particular in the grave's construction, and that they probably obtained their information from this identical man."

Archie Eaton made plans to travel to Cincinnati to tell his uncle John what had happened, not realizing that about the same time Scott's body had been discovered missing from its grave, John Harrison was standing over his father's body at the medical college.

Carter Harrison was eating dinner when he was informed of his father's grave being disturbed. Carter immediately dispatched to the site of the grave an old servant, J. Myer, who had been employed by his father for thirty years. Myer soon confirmed the terrible affair and Carter dispatched a telegram to his brother Benjamin, telling of the desecration.

*"Fathers' grave has been robbed. I shall leave for Cincinnati on the first train. Come here immediately."*

Carter made his way to the train depot to go to Cincinnati. There he met Archie and together they boarded the train to begin the search for Scott's body.

# Chapter Five

*"The law in this state is such that no one can consider themselves safe from the dissectors after death."*
-<u>Cincinnati Daily Times</u>  May 31, 1878

It has been estimated that between 1811 and 1881 in Ohio alone  over five thousand bodies  were resurrected from their graves for the purpose of medical dissection.[19] Though some places, such as England were creating laws to provide a legal supply of bodies to the medical schools, Ohio maintained  anti-dissection laws that made a difficult situation worse.   By 1846, robbing a body from its grave was punishable by a fine of one thousand dollars, and a six month jail sentence.  This did not stop students or doctors from procuring bodies from graveyards. It was considered by some of the students as a rite of passage into the medical field. For others it was an adventure to be talked about later, and a way to impress the ladies.

The following story is that of Dr. Joseph Nash McDowell, Professor of Anatomy and Physiology in the Medical Department of the Cincinnati College from 1835 to 1839. It is a perfect example of the exaggerated tales told by doctors of the time to dazzle their young students.

Dr. McDowell was ever alert to the chance of getting material for his classes. Once he was told of a girl who had died of an unusual disease. He was determined to dissect the body. He took two students with him and exhumed the corpse, then took it to the college. Word leaked out somehow about what he had done. The girl's friends decided to call on the college, get the body back, and repay the doctor for his actions. Dr. McDowell decided it would be prudent to hide the body. He went to the college about 11 p.m.; the place was vacant and silent. He went to the dissecting room with a small lantern, threw the girl's body over one shoulder, and started to carry it upstairs to hide it in the rafters.

*"I had ascended one flight of stairs when out went my lamp. I laid down the corpse and re-struck a light. I then picked up the body, when out went my light again. I felt for a match in my pocket, when I distinctly saw my dear, old mother*

who had been dead these many years, standing a little distance off, beckoning me.

"In the middle of the passage was a window; I saw her rise in front of it. I walked along close to the wall, with the corpse over my shoulder, and went to the top-loft and hid it. I came down in the dark, for I knew the way well; as I reached the window in the passage, there were two men talking, one had a shotgun, the other a revolver. I kept close to the wall and slid down the stairs. When I got to the dissecting-room door, I looked down the stairs into the hallway: there I saw five or six men lighting a lamp. I hesitated a moment as to what I should do, as I had left my pistols in my pocket in the dissecting-room when I took the body. I looked in the room, as it was my only chance to get away, when I saw my spirit mother standing near the table from which I had just taken the corpse. I had no light, but the halo that surrounded my mother was sufficient to enable me to see the table quite plainly.

"I heard the men coming up the stairs. I laid down whence I had taken the body and pulled a cloth over my face to hide it. The men came in, all of them armed, to look at the dead. They uncovered one body, - it was that of a man, the next a man; then they came to two women with black hair, - the girl they were looking for had flaxen hair. They then passed me, one man saying: 'Here is a fellow who died in his boots; I *guess he is a fresh one.'*

*"I laid like marble. I thought I would jump up and frighten them, but I heard a voice, soft and low, close to my ear, say, 'Be still, be still.' The men went over the building, and finally downstairs. I waited a while, then slipped out. At the next street corner, I heard the three men talking; they took no notice of me, and I went home. We dissected the body, buried the fragments and had no further trouble.[80]*

Some doctors were not so lucky. Professor John T. Shotwell, who taught anatomy at the Medical College of Ohio, could attest to the dangerous nature of the business. He was called Well-shot by his students because of being shot at and hit, but not seriously hurt, during one of his body snatching expeditions.

As more students turned to the medical profession there became a regular demand for 'subjects' for dissection. Doctors became tired of risking not only their lives, but a prison sentence as well, to retrieve dissecting material. Students weren't much better acting as body-snatchers. They had a tendency to dig up the whole grave, open the coffin and leave it uncovered. This was quite time consuming and alerted the town of the crime. The end result was that it became even harder to obtain bodies and brought considerable heat on the local colleges. Something had to be done.

In desperation the Medical College of Ohio sent word out that the college would be interested in buying bodies for their ever growing number of students.

Thus the profession of resurrectionist was born and flourished. In time, these men became so good at their 'art' that it was impossible to tell that a grave had been disturbed, even in cases when it was known to have been opened.

Newspapers made many guesses as to how this was done. Some stated that the robbers were digging from twenty to thirty feet away and tunneling to the body, although people with common sense knew this wasn't possible. It would have taken days to dig through that much hard earth. So how was it really done?

Many times it began before the body was even buried. When the family and friends would gather around the burial coffin, there might be an extra 'mourner' who would make sure everything was clear for digging. Sometimes the 'mourner' would mark the spot to make it easier to find later.

The *Cincinnati Times* gave the people of the day a good idea of how the resurrectionist worked.

### *Resurrectionists*
### *How Their Shocking Trade is Plied*

*"The detectives say that they can easily distinguish the work of a professional body-snatcher from that of the novice.*

*"A new man, or an apprentice will, at first, work twice as hard as necessary. The first few graves he robs he takes the trouble of entirely opening. The professional merely digs a small*

hole down to the head of the coffin, at an angle of 60 degrees or more. The embryo ghouls opens the whole top of the coffin, and sometimes takes the trouble to unscrew the lid and to carefully screw it down again! The professional, when he digs down to the head of the coffin, takes a large augur and bores a number of holes close together across the coffin lid, about eighteen inches from the top. Then he knocks in the lid, ties a rope around the neck of the body, and with a few dexterous pulls, jerks it out of its resting place and lands it on top of the ground. The clothes are torn off and placed back in the empty coffin, and the hole covered up.

"The body snatchers seldom or never steal the grave clothes. He deserves no praise for his forbearance. It is too risky. The chances of getting caught are too great. One instance is known where a resurrectionist dressed up in the clothes taken from a body he had stolen, and was detected wearing them in the house of God. The stolen body was that of a brother of the preacher, and when the latter recognized the garments he fainted dead away, supposing the same his brother's ghost."

# Chapter Six

*"You expect us to cure you of disease, and yet
deny us the only means of learning how?"*
–<u>Diary of a Late Physician</u> by Samuel Warren

A reporter for the *Cincinnati Commercial* newspaper
entered the headquarters of the Fire Department on
Sixth Street in search of news regarding any recent fires.
After a few words on that subject, Chief Joseph Bunker
asked the reporter if he had heard about the discovery
of John Scott Harrison's body at the Medical College of
Ohio next door.[21]  Bunker then told him what little he
knew.  The reporter thanked him and hurriedly made
his way over to the college.

A few minutes later he saw six men come out of the

college building bearing a plain burial coffin. It was placed in a waiting wagon and immediately driven away. Two of the men seemed to be supporting a larger man, who was deeply agitated. The reporter tried question them about the body, but they refused to talk.

The reporter quickly chased down the wagon bearing the casket and followed it to Estep and Meyer, a funeral home on Seventh Street. He approached the driver, whom he recognized as Thomas Estep.

"Whose body have you got there?" asked the reporter.

"I cannot say." Replied Estep. "My employers have enjoined me not to say anything to anyone on the subject."

"Is it the body of John Scott Harrison?"

"I'm sorry, I'm not at liberty to say anything about it."

Frustrated, the reporter returned to the college and talked to Aquilla Marshall, the janitor.

"I know nothing about the body." Marshall claimed.

"Do you know who brought it to the college?"

"No. I didn't even know that it was here in the first place."

Marshall did admit to the reporter that he felt the violation of respectable graveyards was wrong, and did not think that the faculty would approve of it if they knew. He went on to say that he didn't care what might happen to his own body, but recognized the fact that his relatives might.

"Do you know the names of any body snatchers in

the city?" asked the reporter.

"No, but there are many of them, and they will do anything for money." Marshall answered.

A half hour later the *Commercial* reporter caught up with John Harrison. John apologized for his behavior at the college.

"I'm sorry that we didn't speak before," John stated, "but we had hoped to keep this terrible business quiet, so that those near and dear to our father might not have to hear the miserable story. I am saddened to find that this is impossible." He told the reporter of the many precautions that had been taken to prevent his father being removed from his grave, and the search for Devin's body that led him to his father.

John, as well as Detective Snelbaker and Attorney Harry Cooper, decided to return by train to North Bend to find out if the Harrison grave had indeed been robbed. As they waited at the depot, the train from North Bend arrived with Carter and Archie aboard.

Spying his brother, Carter cried out, "John, they've stolen father's body" in the same instant that John said "I've found father's body." It was a moment of renewed grief for the brothers, tempered with relief in Carter's mind that the body of his father had not been lost to him forever.

# Chapter Seven

<u>*Body-Snatcher*</u> *n. One who supplies the young physicians with that which the old physicians have supplied the undertaker.*
-<u>The Devil's Dictionary</u> by Ambrose Bierce

The police departments of both Cincinnati and North Bend began to bring in known body snatchers for questioning, but they held little hope in solving the case quickly. The fact that a buggy, and not a delivery wagon, had been used to deliver the body on the morning of May 30th, (as reported in the *Cincinnati Enquirer*), led the police to fasten the crime on someone other than the lower class ghouls who usually performed that kind of work.

Patrick Prendiville, a night watchman at the North Bend train depot, told the police that he had seen a buggy drive rapidly down River Road at about one o'clock the morning after Scott's funeral. He had noticed the buggy for two reasons. He knew of no animal in the city that could travel as fast as that horse did, plus the buggy made no noise in running. Prendiville believed that the rims of the wheels had been wrapped with cloth to prevent any noise. There were two men in the buggy, and he heard one speak excitedly to the other as they shot past him. From this testimony the police concluded that the buggy could have contained Scott's body. As Cincinnati was about fifteen miles away, it would have taken the buggy about two hours to reach the city. This would have put the buggy in Cincinnati around three o'clock, about the same time the incident in the alley at the Ohio Medical College occurred.

Thomas Linn was brought to the North Bend police station. Wednesday had been a warm night and there was scarcely any excuse for Linn to be absent from watching Scott's grave. His house was located about 500 yards away from Congress Green, which was the reason he had been hired to watch the grave. Unfortunately Linn's view of the graveyard from his house was blocked by a growth of trees. Linn stated that he had visited the cemetery four times the night before, at 11, 12, 1 and 3 o'clock. He thought that the body must have been taken before his first visit at 11 o'clock. To a query from one of the reporters as to how closely Linn had approached the grave he replied, "Near enough to see that it (the grave) was there."

Linn agreed he might have been careless, but hadn't thought that the body would need much watching, since Devin's body had been stolen from the graveyard only a few days before. "But to tell the truth," Linn said, "if I had imagined for a minute that anyone had been going there with the intention of digging up a body, I wouldn't have gone there for fifty dollars."

The police next took Robert Roundtree into custody. Roundtree had been present at Scott's burial, and had seemed to be unusually curious about how the grave was constructed.. Local opinion held that he was a good-for-nothing character. Although he was a coal shoveler by trade, Roundtree very seldom worked. He had a wife and several children, and it was a mystery to the community how he managed to support them.

While under the influence of liquor Roundtree was a talkative fellow and on several occasions in the past he had let it be known that there was no necessity in a man having to work, that there were easier ways to make a living, and that digging up human remains was one of them. On one instance he was heard to brag that he had lately sold the body of a child for ten dollars. A carriage from one of the medical colleges had met him in Riverdale, and relieved him of his load.

When news of the most recent grave robberies became known a great many people visited Congress Green, among them Robert Roundtree. As he walked past the Harrison inclosure he remarked that he once got $500 for raising a body.  When the gentlemen with him asked what he meant, Roundtree declined to give any further details.  The police arrested Roundtree a few hours later.

Police obtained a search warrant for Roundtree's home in order to look for evidence.  They found nothing suspicious but an old axe, with a piece of hemp cord clinging to it.  The piece of untwisted cord corresponded to the piece of rope which was found in Devin's grave.  It was possible that the axe was used  to break open the box coffin in which Devin was buried.

After his arrest, Roundtree claimed his innocence in a peculiar way.

"I was never offered any money for removing the bodies," he exclaimed, "and would, of course, not do anything of the sort for nothing."

Roundtree aroused further suspicions when he began contradicting himself.  When asked his whereabouts on the night of the grave robbing, he had told the police he had been in bed that night between 8 and 8:30 p.m.  Yet later that same afternoon he complained to one policeman that he was sleepy because he had been out late fishing.  When he was brought in, Roundtree had an injury to the third finger on his right hand.  When asked what had caused it, he stated to Marshal Brown that he had worked at the local coal elevator on Thursday evening and a lump of coal had fallen upon his hand and injured it.  When later questioned by Augustus Devin's brother,  Bernard , Roundtree claimed that a plank from the scaffolding at the elevator had fallen upon his finger and crushed it.

The same day that Roundtree had been brought in for questioning, Inspector Charles Wappenstein, from the Cincinnati police, and Allan Pinkerton, the famous Chicago detective, arrested John Crown.[22]   Crown, alias Crowney, was a brother-in-law of Marshall the janitor. Three well-known loafers from North Bend, 'Doc' Moore, John Mozingo and Hank Garrison, were also questioned.   They disclaimed any knowledge of the grave robbery, but had reputations as 'hangers-on' and a familiarity of the Congress Green cemetery.  All of the suspects were later released for lack of evidence.

Several papers reported that the work looked to be that of a real professional and they further speculated that perhaps it was the work of someone who had studied body snatching from "Old Cunny."

William Cunningham was the bogey man that parents threatened their children with in Cincinnati in the mid to late 1800's.  Called Old Man Dead, The Ghoul and most of all Old Cunny, this giant of an Irishman was the best known resurrectionists in the state from 1855 until his death in 1871.

Old Cunny had an unusual method of transporting the bodies from the cemetery to the colleges.  Rather than put the body in the back of the wagon, and risk being stopped and asked what he might be transporting at that time of night, he would dress the corpse in an old coat, vest and hat and prop it up next to him on the driver's seat.  Cunny would hold the reins in one hand and support the body with the other.   If anyone ventured too near, or if the body started to fall forward, Cunny would slap his companion's face and say "Sit up! This is the last time I am going to take you home when you're drunk. The idea of a man with a family disgracing himself in this way!"[23]

In October 1871 the local papers reported that Cunningham had died. The next day the *Cincinnati Daily Enquirer* reported that Cunny was in the Cincinnati Hospital due to drinking bad whiskey. Cunny reassured all that the reports of his death the day before were in error. He promised to be back in business soon, saying that it was being sadly neglected in his absence. Unfortunately for the medical colleges, William Cunningham passed away on November 2, 1871, a little over a week later; he was 64 years old. A business man to the end he had sold his own body to the Medical College of Ohio. His bereaved widow, a woman once described as a bony, brawny, square-jawed Irish woman with a mouth like an alligator, managed to get an additional five dollars from the college on account of the huge size of her husband's body. The skeleton of Cunny hung in the Museum of the Medical College of Ohio for a number of years in memory of his daring deeds as a resurrectionist for the college.

A reporter for the *Cincinnati Enquirer* interviewed one of Cunny's 'pupils', Charles H. Keeton, of Cincinnati. The reporter described Keeton as "a brawny, broad-shouldered colored man, six feet in his stockings, jet black, with retreating forehead, rough shaggy mustache, straggling whiskers, big horny hands to which the clay of newly-disturbed grave seemed yet to be sticking." Keeton frankly acknowledged that, although he was an expressman during the day, his night profession consisted of body snatching. He justified himself by saying that he bestowed his labors in the interests of science.

"How long have you been in this business?" asked the reporter.

"About eleven years, sir." said Keeton, as he brushed some of the imaginary clay from his hands. He sat on his bed, for he was sick - confined to his room from hemorrhage of the lungs. "I began with Mr. Cunningham, 'Old Cunny' they called him, eleven years ago, and have followed the business every winter since that."

"Does it pay pretty well?"

"Not now. It used to pay, for we got a good price for subjects, but there isn't much money in it now."

"Why don't they pay so much now?"

"Well, sir, the fact is - I don't want to say nothing against anybody, but it appears to me that somebody ain't exactly doing the fair thing by the profession of subject-gathering. I don't 'cuse none of the doctors themselves of going out to get stiffs, but there's something wrong somewhere. The old demonstrators of anatomy at the Colleges wouldn't have stooped to such a thing either, but I think things are changed now. I went to the demonstrator of one College - I ain't going to call any names - in March, and asked him how many subjects they were going to want for the spring session, and he told me he thought they wouldn't want any more, that they had enough on hand. Well, you see, I knew better than that, a long ways better than that, and my private opinion is that that 'ere Demonstrator gets his subjects in some queer sort of way. I don't say that he goes out for 'em himself, but if he doesn't he must have some no 'count men that would as soon rob the grave of a party well connected, and with lots of friends, as any other way. Now, no body-snatcher as has any respect for himself or his calling will do a thing of that sort. There's plenty of material lying 'round and rotting, just rotting, sir, and with no friends to claim it; and there's no reason why the body-snatchers should go 'round stealing bodies of people who have friends, when there are plenty of others they can take without hurting any body's feelings."

"Then you don't think this Harrison robbery was done by one of the regular professionals, eh?"

"No, sir, I don't."

"What do you think about it?"

"Well, I think it was done by robbers - thieves. Mind, I don't call them what works for the aid of science robbers, for taking the body of them as ain't got no friends ain't stealing it, leastwise when you are getting it in aid of medical science. I think them what opened this grave done it mostly for the clothes the dead man wore. Then, of course, when they had the body, thought they might as well sell it. Nobody would take the trouble to go out to North Bend twenty miles, to get a body when they could get plenty of just as good and very much nearer, just as well. Then, too, the grave was cemented up and big stones put in, and it took a great deal of labor to get it out. No, sir; nobody'd go out there just to get the body; at least no professional would. It must have been somebody that wanted the clothes as well as the body, and somebody that wasn't very well up to snuff, neither."

"Then the College has not been buying many this spring?"

"Very few, at least from the reg'lar men that furnishes 'em."

"How many of those are there?"

"Oh, there are half a dozen now. Some of them are new ones at it, though."

"How long have you been at it?"

"It's about 'leven years since I first begun it. I begun with Old Cunny. First he paid me $3 a head; that was while I was learning. Then he gave me $8 a piece, and finally I decided to quit him and go by myself, and so he said he'd give me half, and then we worked together on shares till he died."

"Do you make it a regular business then?"

"Well, I get my living by it in the winter time."

"What do you get for subjects?"

"Well, we used to get about $25 apiece for them, but lately the price somehow got down to $15. The Professors buy some subjects for themselves, and they most always get 'em for about $15."

"How do you usually get the bodies?"

"Well, we generally go out two together and go to the burying ground. We go to the 'poor lots', the Potter's

Field, and when we can find any fresh graves we get the bodies."

"You don't get them from the parts where the better class of people are buried?"

"No. Lots of times Cunny and I have been out together and we'd find a fresh grave on a large lot, and Cunny would always say, 'Come along, honey, we won't take that.' When we'd come through to the part where the graves were close together, and we knew it was the poor lot where the people without any friends are buried, then we'd dig down to the coffin, break it open and put a rope around the neck and pull the body out. I don't do it that way now, though, for it is just as easy to throw all the dirt out. Then, after throwing it out I generally get down and open the coffin and take the body by the waist and lift it out to my partner. He takes it, and gen'ly runs a knife down the back and rips the clothes off and let's 'em drop down. Then we slip the head into a sack, press the knees up against the chest, and slip the body in and tie the sack. That's all there is to it."

"How do you enjoy the work?"

"Well, it wasn't very pleasant at first, of course; but any one gets used to it. It is for the good of science, and I think it is just as right and honorable as for the man what does the dissection. I want to say one thing, though, and that is that the colored people have 'cused me of robbing the graves in their graveyards. I have never done so. I have took up a good many bodies of colored people wot was buried in the 'poor lot', but never any other."

"How many do you suppose you have furnished in your experience as a body-snatcher?"

"Maybe five hundred. I got about forty last winter, but it wasn't a very good winter for it, though."

The reporter concluded from this interview that someone else, someone outside of the ordinary gang of local resurrectionists, was supplying the colleges with bodies.

Keaton died from his illness a month after the interview. He had sold his body to the Ohio Medical College while alive, receiving the usual price of $35. He requested that his skeleton stand next to Cunny's so that he could keep the "ole man" company. His wish was granted.

# Chapter Eight

*"...whoever receives, conceals, or secretes any corpse (removed unlawfully from it's grave)... shall be fined not more than one thousand dollars, or imprisoned not more than six months, or both."*
- <u>Cincinnati Commercial</u> June 1, 1878

Benjamin Harrison arrived at the Cincinnati train depot at 10 p.m. May 30th, where reporters met him.

"What will you do, now that your father's body has been found?" asked one of them.

"Through the kindness of B. F. Strader, a permit has been obtained to entomb my father's body in the old Jacob Strader vault, in Spring Grove Cemetery here in your city. There it will remain until fall when it will be returned to our family burial plot."[84]

"Did you know, sir, of the apologies being forwarded by the college?" asked a reporter from the *Cincinnati Daily Times*.

"I wish you to state, sir, that our family can accept no apologies or explanations from any member of that faculty who has any knowledge or suspicion of who is responsible for this outrageous act. We will accept nothing from them but a clear statement of the case. We do not want any hypocritical sympathy. We want information as to who are the guilty parties."

"And the search for Augustus Devin's body?"

"Nothing that would tend to its recovery shall be left undone. Up to this hour we have obtained no definite knowledge of his whereabouts. Further than that I cannot speak."

About the same time Benjamin arrived in Cincinnati, his brother Carter was swearing out a warrant before Justice of the Peace, Benjamin M. Wright, for the arrest of the janitor of the Medical College of Ohio, Aquilla Marshall. Marshall was arrested on the following warrant on May 30th, 1878.

> *State of Ohio, Hamilton County.*
> *Before me, B. M. Wright, one of the Justice of the Peace of said county, personally came Carter B. Harrison, who being duly sworn according to law, deposes and saith that on or about the 29th day of May, A.D. 1878, at the county of Hamilton and State of Ohio, a party*

whose name is to affiant unknown, the janitor of
the Ohio Medical College, unlawfully and
maliciously did receive, conceal and secrete in a
certain place, to-wit: the Ohio Medical College
Building, the body of John Scott Harrison,
deceased, which said body had by some person to
affiant unknown, unlawfully and maliciously had
been taken and removed from its grave, situated
in the Township of Miami, without lawful
authority, the said janitor then and there at the
time he so aforesaid received and concealed said
body there, knowing the same body to have been,
in the manner aforesaid, unlawfully and
maliciously removed from its grave, as aforesaid,
and further the deponent saith not.

*C. B. Harrison*

*Sworn to and subscribed before me this 30th day
of May, in the county aforesaid.*

*L. Block, J. P.*

*Walter Lacy, Constable*

It should be noted that there was an informality in
the affidavit. The warrant was brought before one
Justice of the Peace, and signed by another. It seems
that Justice Wright used a warrant already signed by
Justice Leopold B. Block, that being the only one
available. This fact would become important at a later
time.

Marshall was arrested and taken to Cell 61 of the
County jail.[25] He was forty-seven years old, with his

black hair just beginning to be sprinkled with gray. Except for sideburns, the balance of his face was close shaven, with a somewhat pugnacious nose and a firm mouth. His eyes had a sharp, wary look.

When the discovery of John Scott Harrison's body in the medical college became a subject of discussion on the streets a party of gentlemen visited the county jail to see the man thought responsible for hiding the body. Marshall was confused as to why such a ruckus was being made over such a common incident as the discovery of a body.

An official asked if he had hauled the body up.

"No, sir, of course not." Marshall answered, with a quick, searching glance at the questioner that betrayed his anxiety.

"Is it part of your duty to hoist them up after they are tied on?"

"No. My duty is in the lower part of the building."

"Don't you ever come up here in the dissecting rooms?"

"Not often. I have men to keep them clean."

"Where were you the morning when the corpse was drawn up?"

"In bed, of course."

"And you don't know anything about it?"

"Don't know anything about it."

"Who, then, did haul it up?"

"Why, the men who brought it here, of course."

"Is that the custom?"

"Yes."

"They come clear up here to the top of the building, do they, and bring it up themselves?"

"Yes, they do."

"How do they get in?"

"The door is always open."

"Now, see here," said the questioner, "do you mean to tell me that you did not do it yourself?"

"Yes, I mean to tell you just that. Why, what do you take me for?"

"Never mind what I take you for. I don't want any scallops about it. I mean business, and I want you to tell me the truth."

"I am telling you the truth." said Marshall.

Marshall was visited that same night by Drs. William W. Seely, P. S. Conner, and Frederick Forchheimer,of the Medical College of Ohio, who told him that they would see that his case was well defended.[26] They also assured Marshall that his family would be well taken care of.[27] As they left, the doctors gave instructions to the guards that Marshall should be furnished with whatever he wanted.

That same night, Constable Lacy, with a number of volunteers, made a second thorough search of the college. They were at first refused admittance by one of the faculty, who claimed that the search warrant did not extend into the night. Lacy, however, said that he was going in no matter what. The professor warned that he had enough students in the place to bar the entrance; Lacy retorted that the students might try their hand at stopping him if they wished. After glancing at the number of men Lacy had brought with him, the professor grudgingly admitted them. Lacy and his men found no sign of Devin, however the Constable carried off the keys to the building that night, so that he could resume the search the next morning.

# Chapter Nine

<u>*Grave*</u> *n. A place in which the dead are laid to await the coming of the medical student.*
-<u>The Devil's Dictionary</u> by Ambrose Bierce

Marshall was brought before Judge Benjamin M. Wright the next morning and placed under a $5000 bond. He was scheduled to appear in court on Thursday, June 6th, at 8:30 a.m. Dr. James T. Whittaker, Professor of Physiology and of Clinical Medicine of Medical College of Ohio, appeared before Judge Wright and made it known that the faculty had collected the money needed to post Marshall's bond.[28] Public opinion of this action was not looked upon as a gesture of kindness by the college for an employee, but as a case of fellow criminals helping their comrade

The *Cincinnati Daily Times* interviewed Dr. Seely on his possible involvement in the body snatching.

"The newspapers have been a little one-sided in the matter," said Seely. "'Tis true that this circumstance is one to be deeply deplored, and none can feel it more sincerely than the Faculty of our College.

"Now, the papers have made it appear that we had a hand in this matter of robbing Mr. Harrison's grave of its dead. The impression given out is that we direct this one or that one to procure such a body, and that under our orders this lamentable affair was carried out. I can assure you that such was not the case. And more, had we known whose body it was that was suspended on that rope, we would have returned it to its grave and said nothing about it.

"'Tis true we must have bodies to work on, but it is not politic to run such risks and we are not in favor of such desecration as that practiced in this instance."

"It must be known who brought the body. It must have been paid for, and those paying can explain the whole mystery," replied the reporter.

"There you are wrong. The body was brought here at night and placed in the chute, and I suppose that had not such a stir been made, we would have been called upon for payment. As it is, the man will not be likely to do so, and we may never know who resurrected it."

Public anger toward Dr. Seely and the Medical College of Ohio began to grow. A group of friends of the Harrison family went to the Grand Hotel to try and convince Benjamin to mob the college.

"I can well understand your exasperation, and feel my share of it." he told them. "But, under the circumstances, my influence would be against anything like mob violence. I would discountenance that as a form of expression of public sentiment unworthy of the occasion. The duty of the community is to see that the law is vindicated, nothing short of that would be satisfactory."

Dr. Marmaduke Wright,a colleague of Dr. Seely's, called on Seely the morning of May 31.[29]

"Dr. Seely, it is your duty to give all the information that you know to the Harrisons in regard to the men who have committed this crime. Not only that, but you must tell the public that you, in no way, approved of the act.[30]

Swayed by his good friend, Dr. Seely agreed to tell the Harrisons of his suspicions of who might have committed the crime.

"At the very least I might be able to give him a clue that might lead to the arrest of one or more criminals."

Delighted, Dr. Wright immediately rushed to tell the Harrisons of his meeting with Dr. Seely. He hoped that Seely's information would put the college on the right side of the law, and stem the public outcry against it.

He easily found Benjamin Harrison and together they went back to Dr. Seely's office at 118 West Seventh Street. Informed that he was at the college, they went there, located him, and the three of them returned to Seely's office to discuss the matter.

"Doctor," Benjamin said, "I have understood that you are willing to relate to me certain suspicions which you hold against one or more parties, with the view of aiding me in my search for the offenders."

Dr. Seely sat as if ill at ease, and deep in thought.

Benjamin went on. "I would like to not only get my clutches on the riflers of my father's grave, but also on anyone with whom the robbers were in collusion."

Benjamin noticed that the doctor was agitated.

"But, mind," Harrison continued, "if the recital of your suspicions or clue will in any way incriminate yourself, I would prefer that you remain silent."

A long pause followed.

"I have changed my mind." Dr. Seely said, abruptly. "I will not tell you anything."

Dr. Wright was on his feet in an instant.

"This will not do, Dr. Seely." said Wright, surprised by Seely's actions. "You place me in a very embarrassing position by your singular conduct, and I wish you to change your attitude in relation to this matter. Your attitude will throw grave suspicions that you are a party to the crime by your refusal to do your duty as promised."[81]

It was no use.

Benjamin was highly indignant at the end of the interview. Bowing himself from the presence of Dr. Seely, he let it be known that he was not done with him.

# Chapter Ten

*"Could every grave in Ohio be opened and the empty coffins counted, there would be such a storm raised..."*
-<u>Cincinnati Enquirer</u> June 15, 1878

In June of 1879 a reporter from the *Cincinnati Commercial* made a tour of the local public cemeteries to ascertain their conditions and to learn what precautions were being taken to prevent the bodies from being exhumed. The paper thought that in view of the excitement caused by the theft of John Scott Harrison's body, even this aspect of the story would be of interest. The developments of the last few days had made everyone leery of consigning their loved ones to burial grounds. If cemented walls, stoned weights and watchmen couldn't save Scott's grave from being desecrated, what could?

The reporter opened his article by painting a picture of those lonely graveyards, and what could happen to the remains of loved ones during the night:

> *"It was not pleasant, to put it mildly, for one to mediate... that the body of the mother who had borne and nourished him and whom he loved and revered was liable to be hooked under the chin and dragged from its resting place, and carted through the streets naked by ruffians, and hauled up the 'well' in the medical college, and exposed to the knife of careless and reckless young students, who carved the sacred remains with pipe in mouth and the ready jest and laugh on tongue."*

St. Johns Cemetery was located near Chester Park, in the village of Clifton, north of Cincinnati. The Superintendent was Henry Von Wahide, a very efficient and affable gentleman, who had succeeded the old superintendent two years before.[32] When the *Commercial* reporter visited, he noticed that no human guards were posted to guard the approximately 35,000 corpses buried there. Two Newfoundland dogs, by the names of Noble and Cario, kept the night watch. They had been trained from puppyhood to their business and were naturally grim and ugly to all but their master and his assistants.

"These sentinels can not be bought up or frightened." Von Wahide told the reporter, clearly referring to what happened with Linn, the watchman over Harrison's grave. "As soon as the gates are closed at night not the nearest neighbor dare enter the grounds, or attempt to. If they got inside, the dogs would tear them to pieces. We have never had any trouble here, and within my experience, a grave has never been disturbed. If a person is buried here who died of some peculiar or strange disease or when we get a rumor that the doctors would like to get the body, then we go on watch for a week or two ourselves. But the dogs are better than human watchmen, for they know no fear. They want no sleep, and they can not be bought off." Besides Noble and Cario, the superintendent had another Newfoundland he was training and a Spitz which could make enough noise to wake the dead themselves.

Spring Grove, located in Cincinnati, was considered to be one of the finest cemeteries in America, and perhaps the world. Adolph Strauch was the superintendent. There the reporter found that a patrol traversed the grounds every night from dark until daylight. The guard consisted of three men who were armed with revolvers and rifles and who were instructed to shoot anyone they found on the grounds after dark.

"I tell them 'If you see a man in the cemetery after the gates are closed, or a reasonable time has expired, ask no questions and hesitate not at all. Shoot the person at once," said Strauch, adding that he knew of no attempts ever being made to resurrect any bodies at Spring Grove.[33]

Wesleyan Cemetery was already very old by 1878 and very well filled. It was located on Colerain Pike, near the Cincinnati, Hamilton and Dayton Railroad, and was situated in the midst of a flourishing and rapidly increasing population.[34] The reporter found no watchmen guarding the 25 acres of burial ground. John S. Baldwin, who had held the position of Wesleyan Superintendent for twenty years, insisted that no guards were needed with the cemetery being so close to the city. Besides, he claimed most of the bodies being taken were out of smaller country graveyards.

After visiting three other cemeteries the reporter ended his article by stating that if any good, healthy and reasonably discreet body-snatcher wanted to get a body out of any of the large cemeteries about the city they would, eight times out of ten, find little trouble in doing so.

*"How many have been snatched out by a hook under the jaw can not be told. Perhaps few, perhaps many, but in spite of what the Superintendent of all three grounds say about dogs, guards and precautions, it is a fact that many and many a dark story is told of the work of resurrectionists in these graveyards, and of the 'stiffs' that have been carted into the city by night along Spring Grove avenue or down Warsaw pike."*

With the publication of this and other related stories, the public began to panic. People were no longer sure whether their relatives were still in their graves, or had found their way to the "chute". The papers reported that people had started opening graves, of their recently interred loved ones, only to find them empty.

One incident involved two graves of little children being opened. The infants' graves had not been disturbed, but the appearance of the little bodies was so terrible that it served as a caution to those planning to do the same thing. The graves were full of water, as were the tiny coffins themselves. One baby, partly decayed, floated up against the glass coffin front. In her anxiety to see if her child's body was still there, the dead child's mother had wiped the dirt and dampness from the glass front herself and looked in at the ghastly sight. "It did not make a pretty picture." said one who saw it.

The citizens of Indiana began to worry about whether the tomb of former president William Henry Harrison might be broken into and his remains taken - a fear well founded after the snatching of his son's body. William H. Harrison was still held in high regard for his role as the first governor of the Indiana Territory. The Harrison tomb consisted of a plain vault located on the summit of a hillock, rising out of North Bend, Ohio, a mere three hundred yards from the Indianapolis, Cincinnati and Lafayette train depot. The hillock was, for the most part, covered with thick undergrowth, and immediately surrounding the vault were a few small evergreens. The roof of the vault proper stood only three feet above ground, and the chamber and different apartments were entirely beneath the surface of the hill. No letters were inscribed on the tomb, and not the slightest sign marked the last resting place of a man who once held the highest office in the United States.[35]

Around the Harrison family plot an iron picket fence had been built years ago. Outside of this fence were the remains of old pioneers and neighbors. The burying ground was a modest one, possessing only a few monuments. Tall shrubbery made the place pleasant, but it also made it very dark and lonely after nightfall. This was just the sort of place resurrectionists liked, with the darkness and cover affording them some protection from being detected.

A committee from Lawrenceburg, Indiana, headed by Captain J. F. Vaughn, visited North Bend on May 31. They carried instructions to pledge the services of their city in erecting a handsome monument over the grave of President William H. Harrison provided the grave was removed from North Bend to Greendale Cemetery in Lawrenceburg.[36] This hint that perhaps Indiana was better equipped to ensure that the dead president's body was never disturbed was taken as an insult by the Ohio born Harrison family and the offer refused. William Henry Harrison remained where he had been placed by his family 37 years previously.[37]

On Friday, May 31, 1878 John Scott Harrison's body was taken to Jacob Strader's family vault in Spring Grove Cemetery. Situated upon a hill near the center of the cemetery, the Gothic brown Connecticut sandstone chapel and vault had been completed in 1858 by architect and builder James G. Batterson of Hartford. The structure, 25 feet wide and 23 feet deep, contained 26 catacombs. The catacombs were situated below the floor of the vault, and already contained the remains of nine members of the Strader family. Into these catacombs the body of Scott was gently lowered.

# Chapter Eleven

*"Doctor Bartholow admits that the resurrection men with whom he deals with are unscrupulous scoundrels only fit for the state prison, but he intimates that he shall keep on dealing with them all the same."*
-New York <u>Times</u> June 6, 1878

As a move to gain public sympathy, Dr. Roberts Bartholow, Dean of the Medical College of Ohio, handed the following statement to the press on the morning of June 1.

*"The Faculty of the Medical College of Ohio, in common with the rest of the community, heard*

with deep regret that the grave of Hon. J. Scott Harrison had been violated, and that the body of this eminent and respected citizen had been found in the Medical College Building.

"It is merely justice to the Faculty to state that they were entirely ignorant of what had transpired in the College building on the night in question. It is hardly necessary to say that if they had been aware of the purpose of the resurrectionists, the public would have been spared the dreadful details of yesterday. Occurrences of this kind bring such odium on the dissection of the human bodies as to render it more and more difficult to procure subjects, and greatly enhances the price of anatomical material. It is the interest of the Faculty, therefore, to render the practice of dissection as little repulsive as possible.

"Unjust legislation is, in part, responsible for the occurrences of such outrages as that of yesterday. Dissection is not lawful, and yet anatomical knowledge is required of all who practice medicine and surgery. Suits for malpractice are constantly before the Courts, and physicians and surgeons are cast into damages for a lack of that anatomical knowledge which the law deny them an opportunity to obtain. It is true our Legislature a few years ago passed an act permitting the use of dissection of the bodies of strangers and paupers, provided no friends or relatives interposed an objection. This restriction rendered the law practically inoperative. The horror of yesterday should now awaken a proper public sentiment on the subject of dissection of human bodies, and those who die in public institutions and are buried at the public expense should be devoted to the study of anatomy.

"Under existing circumstances, bodies necessary for the instruction of medical students must be stolen. Unfortunately, the men engaged in so disreputable and hazardous an occupation are rather unscrupulous as to the means resorted to and as to cemeteries invaded. At the Medical College of Ohio, with an attendance of more than three hundred students, it is obvious that a large number of 'subjects' must be provided to insure adequate instruction in the important subject of anatomy - the very groundwork of a medical education.

"A very great misconception seems to exist as regards the part taken by the Faculty and their assistants in procuring the material for dissection. The men engaged in the business of procuring subjects, are, of course, unknown to the Faculty: they bring the material to the College, receive the stipulated price, and disappear as mysteriously as they came. In the case of Hon. J. Scott Harrison, it seems to have been brought by the resurrectionist on his own responsibility, and the poor janitor, whom it is sought to punish, had no part in, or knowledge of, the transaction.

"In the search for motives which determined the stealing of Mr. Harrison's body, it is alleged that the doctors had a wish to ascertain the cause of death, because it had been so sudden. It is scarcely necessary to say that the explanation already given is the true one - that a resurrectionist, unknown to us, who was probably short of funds, took this means to replenish his exchequer."

*Roberts Bartholow, M. D.*
*Professor of the Theory and Practice of Medicine and of Clinical Medicine, Dean of the Faculty*

# Chapter Twelve

*"What can we do with the bodies of our loved and lost ones to save them from the ignominy of the 'chute and windlass and dissecting knife of the Medical College?"*
-Cincinnati Commercial June 1, 1878

Until this time the Harrison family had acted with grace and calm over the situation. But when the account of the Ohio Medical College became public, it outraged Benjamin.

He countered at a press conference that the faculty had to have known that his father's body was there.

"The muscle which covers the carotid artery had been carefully pushed away, the artery cut, the blood removed and the preserving fluid injected preparatory to a perfect and complete dissection. This must have been done by the officials of the College themselves, and not the janitor or subordinate, as they intimate."

He then handed the press an open letter of his own for them to publish, which the papers promptly did.

*Grand Hotel Cincinnati, Oh. June 1.*
*To the Citizens of Cincinnati:*

*"I did not suppose when called to your city by a message - the most shocking and horrible ever sent to a son - that I should have occasion to address you except to thank you for your solicitous kindness and sympathy. That burden is heavy upon me this morning.*

*"I can only say for the children of your friend, thank you, thank you, God keep your precious dead from the barbarous touch of the grave robber, and you from that taste of hell which comes with the discovery of a father's grave robbed and the body hanging by the neck like that of a dog, in the pit of a medical college.*

*"But the purpose of this card is not to make my acknowledgments for kindness received, but rather to fix, if I can, the responsibility for this outrage where it ought ultimately to rest.*

*"We have been offered through the press the sympathy of the distinguished men who constitute the faculty of the Ohio Medical College. I have no satisfactory evidence that any of them knew whose body they had; but I have the most*

*convincing evidence that they are covering the guilty scoundrel. While they consent to occupy this position, their abhorrence is a pretense, and their sympathy is cant and hypocrisy.*

*"Who can doubt that if the officers of that institution had desired to secure the arrest of the guilty party, it would have been accomplished before night on Thursday. The bodies brought there are purchased and paid for by an officer of the college. The body-snatcher stands before him and takes from his hand the fee for his hellish work. He is not an occasional visitant. He is often there, and it is silly to say that he is unknown. After being tumbled like dung into that chute by the thief, someone inside promptly elevates the body, by a windlass, to the dissecting room. Who did it, gentlemen of the Faculty? Your janitor denied that it had been upon your dissecting tables - but the clean incision into the carotid artery, the thread with which it was ligatured, the injected veins, prove him a liar. Who made the incision and injected that body, gentlemen of the Faculty? The surgeons who examined his work say he was no bungler. What has your demonstrator of anatomy to say about this? While he lay upon your table, the long white beard, which the hands of infant grandchildren had often stroked in love, was rudely shorn from his face. Have you so little care of your college that an unseen and unknown*

man may do all this: who took him from the table
and hung him by the neck in the pit? Was it to
hide it from friends or to pass his body in your
pickling vats for fall use? For a reliable informant
states that an order had gone out to gather bodies
against your winter term. Your secretary had said,
and I can prove it over his denial, that he thought
he could name the man who did it. But he
refuses my just demand, that he should do so. I
denounce that man who thinks he knows the
guilty party, and will not aid my search, as the
brother of that one who drew my father by the
feet through broken glass and dirt from his
honored grave. Have you advised him,
gentlemen of the Faculty, that he ought to tell?
Or did a change of purpose on this subject come
from a conference with you? You profess to the
public that you are extremely careful and
solicitous that private graveyards shall not be
violated. Do you expect to foster a careful spirit
in your grave robbers by covering them and
making yourselves party to the crime when they
violated your pretended instructions? Would you
not give the public better evidence of your
sincerity if you repudiated the men who, in their
own wrong (if it was so), did the deed? I have not
the composure to state my case clearly, but I
think I have said enough. If the faculty would
have us believe them clear of a knowing
participation in this crime, their conduct must be

*conformable to reason. The law and the common sense of mankind hold him who conceals the fruit of a crime, or aids the escape of a criminal, to partake of the original guilt."*

> *Very truly yours,*
> *Benjamin Harrison*

# Chapter Thirteen

*Don't go and weep upon my grave,*
*And think that there I be;*
*They haven't left an atom there*
*Of my anatomie.*
-<u>Mary's Ghost: A Pathetic Ballad</u> by Thomas Hood


As Augustus Devin's body had not yet been found, on June 3 Bernard Devin went to Justice Scwab's office to procure a warrant to search the Medical College of Ohio. A special warrant was granted and given to Inspector Charles Wappenstein who was told to join the investigation.[38] He, along with Benjamin Harrison, his brothers John and Carter, Bernard F. Devin, Constable Samuel Bloom, Detective Edward G. Armstrong from

Cincinnati, and Mr. Cleary from the Pinkerton Agency went to the college to continue the search.

A number of the faculty were present when the group arrived. They were surprised and troubled over the visit. One man complained that too many people were constantly seeking admission to the college who had no right to be shown the building and suggested that the present party might belong to that number. "I'm about tired of having our college invaded by morbid curiosity seekers." he said.

The group thereupon produced the warrant which convinced the faculty that the group was not just there for curiosity's sake. The gentlemen were then told to inspect the building at their leisure. The party then divided into two groups and began a thorough search for the remains of Augustus, whose body they felt sure was in or about the building.

The group led by Constable Bloom stumbled upon a vat which contained a solution for preserving bodies.

The vat was a wooden box, five feet or more long, nearly as wide, and three feet deep. Bloom raised the lid and peered in, but the stench was so overpowering that he staggered back as though he had been dealt a heavy blow.

"I am used to handling stiffs," Bloom said later. "My employment recently with the Coroner made it necessary. But the sight and smell which lifting that lid revealed exceeded anything that ever came under my observation."

Certain that they had found what they were searching

for, Bloom and the others forced themselves to examine the vats contents. The vat was found to contain three bodies, but none were their dead friend. The overpowering smell sickened their bodies and their spirit; they decided to move on to another floor. The other party, led by Benjamin Harrison, descended to the paved open court yard. Here their attention was attracted by the fact that a portion of the brick pavement appeared to be freshly put down. A plumber assured them that he had taken part of it up to repair a pipe. The officers were inclined to believe the story, but Benjamin insisted on digging. The spot was torn up and the ground excavated to the depth of four or five feet, but nothing was found.

Bloom's group met with more success. Upstairs, in an abandoned lumber room, they found a ladder in a closet that led to a hatchway and a hidden garret. Having provided themselves with lanterns from the Gift Fire Engine House nearby, they climbed up the ladder and entered the garret. No flooring covered the open beams, making the search more dangerous. Between the joists, and on the lathe which supported the plaster ceilings of the room below, they found innumerable items of clothing, taken, presumably, from dead bodies. Someone fetched more lanterns and they began to examine the newer clothing. Stepping cautiously from rafter to rafter in the half darkness, Detective Cleary found a black vest that appeared to be less old and dusty than the rest. He showed it to Bernard, who believed it to be a part of the suit in which John Scott Harrison had been buried in. Encouraged by this find the men continued the hunt. They eventually found a bundle that contained the rest of the missing garments, including a blackcoat and pants and a suit of red flannel underwear.

On recovery of these items, the finders hastily returned to the hall below, where they asked the Harrisons to identify the clothing. All three agreed instantly that the articles were those in which their father had been buried. At this moment Dr. Seely, and Thomas Ackley Logan, a Cincinnati attorney, approached to find out what was going on. Seeing the pile of clothing, Dr. Seely bent over it absent-mindedly and began to pick off the gray hairs that were stuck to the suit. This bit of disrespectful nonchalance was too much for Benjamin. Fist clenched, he stepped menacingly towards the doctor, and told him to get out. Dr. Seely withdrew rather hastily. Benjamin remarked that he now had ample proof that the doctors were all liars, since someone connected with the college had to have thrown his father's clothes in the garret.

Later that same evening Benjamin had a conversation with a reporter from the *Cincinnati Commercial* newspaper.

"The clothes found at the college were my father's beyond a peradventure. It was a suit I had had made and presented to him about a year ago. All of the clothes that were found, the vest, coat, pantaloons, undershirt and drawers, all of them I recognized as belonging to my father.

"The finding of these clothes stowed away up under the rafters of the medical college is in my estimation a cheerful comment on the assertions of the officers of the institution, that they know nothing of the presence of the body in their building. This is an emphatic denial of the janitor's story that the body was not taken out of the shaft by *attaches* of the college. It was taken out and stripped, and then, when we got upon the track, it was placed in the shaft to avoid detection. In my opinion the robbery of my father's grave was specially ordered, that that particular body was wanted, and that men were hired to get it and paid especially for that job."

Benjamin swore that he would search for those responsible until he found them, even if it took years. He added that every faculty member would be testifying in front of the Grand Jury, where they would either have to tell the truth, or perjure themselves.

"I'll tell you one thing, I am not as anxious to bring the body-snatchers to justice as I am to fasten the responsibility of the desecration upon the Faculty of the College."

He then excused himself. "I have to go back to Indianapolis for pressing business, but I plan to return and remain in the city with my brothers until some results are obtained."

Benjamin left for Indianapolis by train later that night. He had to prepare himself to give the keynote address to the State Convention Republicans of Indiana at the Metropolitan Theater in Indianapolis at ten o'clock Wednesday morning.

The day of the speech, all eyes were on Benjamin. Everyone knew what had recently happened to the Harrison family. They wondered if he was strong enough to carry on.

He was. His speech was received with enthusiasm and he ended it by saying, "I have spoken here today under circumstances that have sadly tried me. I did not know whether I should have been able to serve you today. I thank you for the cordial manner in which you have received me and the patience you have shown me."

Immediately after his speech Benjamin started back to Cincinnati.

# Chapter Fourteen

*"(Marshall's) case was set for eight o'clock, and in
spite of the fact that the hour was that in which a
late pillow or coffee and the morning paper are
more enjoyed by the average Cincinnatian than
attendance upon a Justice's court, the little
courtroom was crowded..."*
-<u>Cincinnati Daily Enquirer</u> June 7, 1878

On June 6, the trial of the janitor, Aquilla Marshall,
was set before Judge Wright in the Magistrates Court.
The office was a little tucked up place on the north side
of Sixth Street, just east of Walnut, a little more than a
block from the scene of the discovery of the body of
John Scott Harrison. Marshall was arraigned for trial on

the charge of "unlawfully receiving and maliciously secreting the body of John Scott Harrison." Present were Benjamin, John and Carter Harrison, represented by two Cincinnati lawyers Harry L. Cooper and John H. Morton.[39] Marshall and the Medical College of Ohio were represented by Thomas Logan and Harvey E. Randell, of Logan and Randell, Attorneys-at-Law, of Cincinnati.

To make himself an expert in the phenomena of insanity and mental diseases Logan became an enthusiastic medical student. He was so successful that he became almost indispensable in nearly all the celebrated cases involving mental diseases, both in Ohio and adjoining states, and was well known to the medical community.

Logan opened the trial for Marshall by stating that the warrant was "illegal upon its face." Possibly Logan meant that he could argue the validity of the warrant based on the fact that it had been issued by one judge, but signed by another.

"I do not choose to discuss its invalidity, however, for a certain reason, and for the same I have raised no question as to the validity of the warrant under which search was made in the Ohio Medical College for the body of an alleged deceased. The same feeling that prompted me to silence then, prompts me to silence now. It is a feeling of sincere regret at this occurrence. And, yet, those proceedings, if ever the question arises, will be found invalid and illegal.

"This arrest was made on the 30th of last month,"

Logan continued. "On Monday, the Grand Jury, which has cognizance of this case, was convened. It is an open secret that that tribunal has, during the whole of its session, been engaged in as full and thorough an investigation of this affair as its process will admit. Whether or not the particular allegation contained in this warrant has been investigated, of course, none of us are permitted to say. All we can say is that it is within the jurisdiction of that Grand Jury. I bow to that jurisdiction and recognize it, and so does the defendant at the bar, and those who were with him, although not named in the warrant, that have been connected with this affair by public rumor and gossip.

"Out of respect to the tribunal now lawfully convened, these gentlemen, together with this defendant, who have been implicated in the charge, have chosen to submit in silence to the manifold, unjust, and in some degree inaudible slanders that have been brought up against them. They have felt that a time will arrive when it shall be proper for them to speak, and when they do speak, they feel assured that this community will be assured that those gentlemen who are now most actively engaged in this prosecution, will be ashamed to have so far allowed themselves to be carried away, as to have made insinuations that will hereafter be proven to have been utterly groundless.

"In view, therefore, of the lawful body now in session, which has entire jurisdiction in the matter, I do not propose at this time to enter into the details of the case. On the contrary, I now waive an examination and consent that the defendant shall be bound over to the Grand Jury."

Benjamin Harrison was astounded. Without an examination, he would have no opportunity to question the medical faculty himself in the matter of his father's body being found at the college. He asked the court if he might speak.

"I recognize the right of the defendant to waive an examination and to let his case go to court without a preliminary investigation of the facts involved. Yet, we had come here this morning in the expectation of having this whole manner examined into in the light of day, so that if any injustice had been done by any insinuations to any of those gentlemen to whom council has referred, it might be cleared up here. I may say now, that I came here to have all the gentlemen connected with that faculty brought before your Honor, and if the gentleman had not put them upon the witness stand himself I intended to do so, and to go through the entire business, giving them a fair opportunity here, under oath, and in the presence of their fellow citizens, to disclose what they have to say as to their participation in this infamous crime. I have no power to do that now. I accept the statement from the gentlemen that he does feel sympathy with us in this infamous outrage which had been perpetrated upon our feeling, but I think the day will never come when any of us will feel regret, and much less shame, for any action we have taken in this matter. On the contrary, I state here that these gentlemen have never shown any disposition to throw the burden of guilt where it belongs. It is not appropriate that I shall state this here, but there will be a time and place when, before the public, and not in a secret tribunal, they shall all have opportunity to tell what they know about this horrid deed.

"We feel in this transaction that we are not acting simply for ourselves, but the interest in this matter of horrid recklessness in violating the best feelings of the human heart extends to the whole community. We feel that we are standing not simply for ourselves, to redress our own feelings, or prosecuting for private grievances, but for that which is public scandal and public infamy."

Logan stood before the court and responded.

"I can pardon the gentleman now, as I have heretofore pardoned him and those connected with him in blood and sympathy, the great heat and warmth which has been displayed. No man will go farther than myself in deprecating the violation of a private and respected grave, and in the protestations of sympathy to these gentlemen, under the circumstances which they found themselves placed by the discovery of the remains of their dead. If, upon discovery certain steps had been taken, and certain offers of assistance had been invoked and accepted, all this trouble and scandal might have been avoided."

Benjamin turned toward Logan.

"Will you permit me one word?" he asked.

"Certainly, sir." Logan replied.

Benjamin addressed the bench.

"Since Mr. Logan has alluded to this matter, I must

say that, upon my arrival here, I was waited upon by a member of the Faculty whom I shall always esteem for his kindness and sympathy. He said that Dr. Seely, of the Faculty, had expressed a willingness to give to us the name of the man who had robbed us of our father's body.

"This gentleman, and myself, drove to Dr. Seely's residence and told him the object of our visit. Dr. Seely then went back on what he had said to that gentleman, and refused to give us the name of the man whom he believed, although he had no positive proof, to be guilty, saying that he feared that would involve himself in trouble if he mentioned his belief and suspicion. He further inquired of me what I thought his duty was in the premises. I refused to stand in the relation of a legal adviser to him, and said, as a lawyer, if he had any criminal complicity in this case, he ought not to speak to me about it at all."

Logan once again addressed the court.

"I am glad that, at this early stage of the proceedings, I am able to set Dr. Seely right. If General Harrison, upon finding his father's body, had requested the assistance of the faculty, if he had not been so far controlled by what was, perhaps, the natural impulse of the moment when the unfortunate incident occurred, he would have found that nowhere in this community, and nowhere in this country, would he or his brothers meet with more cordial sympathy than from the faculty for what had happened.[10]

"Yet, how were the Faculty heralded the very next

morning after this transaction? They found themselves wood cutted in the press in this city, they found themselves denounced and the public mind arrayed against them before they had been asked to plead to the charge, yes or no. They were branded as criminals, and were held up in this community where they have passed their lives, and were recognized as honored members of society, and found themselves branded overnight as criminals of the darkest and deepest kind.

"It was under very peremptory instructions that Dr. Seely refused to make any statements in the manner, and I venture that General Harrison, as a lawyer, would not at any other time have condemned him for doing so. It was not his duty, upon conjecture and suspicion, to give up to the elements that were aroused against him, the name of a man against there was no positive proof. Dr. Seely was entirely justified in law, morals and ethics, under those circumstances, in refusing to disclose any name to which only a slight suspicion was attached. Under my advice, they of the faculty have submitted in silence to all the calumny and slander so far heaped upon them.

"I understand that General Harrison invited the bringing of a civil suit, and expresses a wish to have the matter thoroughly tried. He may yet have an opportunity to defend his position in a civil suit."

Benjamin answered briefly and feelingly, citing the circumstances of the finding of the body of his father.

"I am sorry, but Dr. Seely refused to give me any names, therefore this course of action alone remained for me to pursue. The entire affair was an outrage, such as never before perpetrated. My father was brought to their college and found there, while searching for another body, in such a condition as to drive reason from its throne. The community is also outraged. That my father's carotid artery was severed; an injection was made, his venerable beard shorn off, and his body found in that horrid chute is enough to make anyone believe that the Faculty is guilty of this crime. Had they given us any satisfaction there would not have been any bitter feelings. They, by shielding the guilty ones, have made themselves just as liable.

"There is no further need for argument, as there is no legal question at issue. I would not have spoken a word had not Mr. Logan made the remark he did, announcing that he proposed to waive examination." he concluded. "The only duty of the Court is now clear. You must fix the amount of bail of Marshall's appearance before the Court of Common Pleas. I thank the people of Cincinnati for the sympathy they have shown me."

Logan again stood. "I agree with General Harrison that if a man willfully and knowingly shields an avowed criminal to save him from punishment, that man is just as guilty. I will not allow, however, that any of the Faculty has done this. On the contrary, they merely did what their rules and regulations in such matters compel them to do, and that the bitter feeling against Dr. Seely is wrong. Thank you, your Honor."

Judge Wright looked down at the lawyers. "Sitting

here as an examining Court, it is my duty to bind the defendant over to the present or next term of the Criminal Court. If any of you would suggest the amount of bail, I will fix it so."

Morton stood. "On behalf of General Harrison, I suggest that the bail be at the same figure as fixed at the time of Mr. Marshall's arrest."

Logan disagreed. "I think that, as the amount is too excessive, it might be reduced."

"I think otherwise." said Judge Wright. "Bail is fixed at $5000."

The Medical College of Ohio Faculty promptly furnished the bail.

# Chapter Fifteen

*"As there is a great demand on the part of medical colleges for bodies for anatomical purposes, physicians (should) donate their bodies after death... Perhaps they could be induced to contribute the bodies of their families to the cause of science."*
-Indianapolis Journal June 20, 1878

The members of the Faculty of the Medical College of Ohio were summoned before the Grand Jury to testify as to their knowledge of the resurrecting of the body of Scott and its transfer to the dissecting rooms of that institution. Since it was impossible to get access to the verbal testimony given to the Grand Jury, resourceful newspaper reporters interviewed the Professors as they exited the courtroom. They found the Professors more than willing to talk. From these witnesses the *Cincinnati Commercial* reported the following facts:

1) "That the Faculty of the Ohio Medical College, like the Faculties of similar institutions in Cincinnati and other cities of the country, have contracts with certain persons to supply them with cadavers for dissection and anatomical demonstration. These men make it a business, not only supplying the medical college here, but those of other cities, and especially those in smaller places, like Fort Wayne and Ann Arbor, where it is next to impossible to obtain bodies for the dissecting room from other sources.

2) "It is part of the contract with the resurrectionists that they shall not molest private burying grounds, or the bodies of those whose surviving friends feelings would be shocked and outraged by the discovery that the graves had been rifled. The Faculty are not able to determine whether the bodies supplied to them are taken from public or private grounds, but they deplore any invasion of the former for the important reason if no other, that in increases the difficulties and the cost of obtaining subjects for the dissecting table. If the resurrectionists violate their contracts in this particular, and disregard the advice of the Faculty, they do it at their own peril,

*and will not be shielded, if discovered, by the Faculty.*

*3) "It is also a part of the contract with the resurrectionists, at least in the case of the Ohio Medical College, that they shall not only place the cadaver in the dissecting room, but shave the face if there be a beard, cut the hair, and inject the arteries and veins with the substance used in preserving the body. In other words, they must prepare it for the purpose of the demonstrator or the student of anatomy.*

*4) "In the case of Mr. Harrison, at the time the body was taken to the dissecting room, none of the members of the Faculty were in the building, or aware that it had been placed there. It was prepared by the resurrectionist precisely as all others are prepared, including the injection of the arteries - a simple process, easily taught, and in which all professional 'body-snatchers' are proficient. So, far from being privy to the disinterment of Mr. Harrison's body, the Faculty are not even now positively certain by whom it was exhumed and brought to the College, though they suspect it to have been done by a man whose name was given to the Grand Jury to facilitate inquiry. The reason why the Faculty do not positively know the man is that there are several persons engaged in the business, any one of whom might have undertaken the perilous enterprise. The discovery was made before the resurrectionist appeared to demand pay under contract for the body, and of course after that he was careful to keep out of the way or say or do anything whereby he might be identified.*

*5) "The Faculty deny emphatically that there has been any effort at concealment on their part, or any prevarication.    The body came into possession of the College in the ordinary way that cadavers are obtained, and without any collusion on their part, individually or collectively, with the resurrectionists to obtain the body of Mr. Harrison, nor would it have it been received had any of the Professors who knew that gentleman when living had been present at the time it was place in the dissecting room, and recognized it.*

*6) "As to the body of J. Scott being found in the "dead shaft" there is nothing new about it, all bodies are left dangling there, previous to being brought to the dissecting room."*

The citizens were shocked to read this account of what was taking place before the Grand Jury.  To some it seemed that Cincinnati was the center of a prosperous body-snatching business.  It was unpleasant enough that resurrectionists supplied local colleges with bodies for dissection, but to ship them off to other cities, even other states, was hard to believe.

In a related story the *Cincinnati Times* published an article telling of how bodies were prepared for shipment to other cities, and the money that could be made by resurrectionists.

"*After the body is taken from the coffin and the clothes removed, it is wrapped in a coarse bag or sack, and tumbled into a conveyance which is always waiting. If the cadaver is intended for a distant institution it is taken to some quiet place, generally an outhouse or barn, where it is crammed into a box or barrel, and sawdust or straw packed around it. Sawdust is preferred because it absorbs the odoriferous fluid that might otherwise leak out and excite suspicion. The 'stiff' is seldom shipped from the town or village where it was stolen. A neighboring place is generally selected as a shipping point.*

"*Body snatching pays. If it did not, men would not follow it. 'Subjects' command different prices, according to the demand for anatomical material... A fat male subject is hated alike by body-snatchers and medical students. It weighs heavier, occasions more trouble and spoils quicker than a thin, spare cadaver. The latter, consequently, commands a god deal more money. besides, the surplus flesh to be cut away and gotten rid of, makes dissection much more difficult to the students. Dead children are seldom wanted, and body-snatchers are cautioned about stealing them. They are not accepted if under twelve years of age. Twelve to eighteen-year old 'stiffs' bring from $8 to $15. Once in a* *while the leaders of the ring conspire together to increase the retail price of cadavers. In other words, they get a corner on 'stiffs' and run the price up to $45 and $50. But the average price is $30."*

Some who read this were not convinced that the resurrectionists were responsible for injecting the embalming fluid into the corpses. The general consensus was that the Medical College of Ohio had made up this fact so that they could deny any knowledge of Scott's body being in the college.

But, most importantly, a name had been given to the Grand Jury by one of the witnesses as to who might be responsible for the resurrection of John Scott Harrison's body. The man the police were searching for finally had a name.

Dr. Charles O. Morton.

John Scott Harrison - President William Henry Harrison's son and father of Benjamin Harrison. Stolen from his final resting place in 1878.

Benjamin Harrison - John Scott Harrison's son, who later became the 23rd President of the United States.

Dr. William W. Seely -
Executive Officer
Medical College of Ohio

Dr. William Clendenin -
Professor of Surgical Anatomy
Miami Medical College

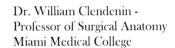

Dr. Marmaduke B. Wright -
Professor of Obstetrics
Medical College of Ohio

Dr. Roberts Bartholow -
Dean
Medical College of Ohio

Thomas Beach
alias
Henri Le Caron
— A British spy —

Gregor Nagele-
Janitor
University of Michigan

Dr. William James Herdman -
Professor of Practical
and Pathological Anatomy
University of Michigan

# Chapter Sixteen

*Give us a furnace, pray,*
*That our poor bodies may consume away*
*From Morton's clutches.*
*Blessed in all the nation*
*Be it's inventor, Refuge Sweet,*
*CREMATION.*
-<u>Cincinnati Daily Enquirer</u> June 24, 1878

The first known appearance of Charles Morton in Cincinnati was on March 1, 1878. On that date he rented rooms from Charles Meyer, owner of Meyer's Pavilion Wine and Beer Saloon and Boarding House at 328 Vine Street. Morton arrived there from Toledo where he had been busy robbing graves.

In 1878 there was no medical school in Toledo, and therefore no local competition there in the resurrection business. Saturday morning, January 19, 1878 Toledo newspapers reported the  startling news that an organized gang of grave robbers had been carrying on successful operations at Forest Cemetery, situated just within the city limits.  On that morning Sexton Edward Radbone found that the grave of Melchior Rall's 12 year old son,  buried on the Wednesday before, had been disturbed.

Digging down to the coffin, he found it empty.  The box in which the casket had been enclosed had been entered by boring several holes in a circle taking out a piece large enough to permit the body to pass through. On the same morning Radbone discovered that the remains of 83 year old Mrs. Lenier, buried the day before, had also been taken.

Police arrested a young man who had been seen loitering around the cemetery for several days  and took him to the Central police station.  At first he claimed that he had no knowledge of the crime but he eventually confessed.  He said that his name was Henry Morton, that he was 16 years of age and that the chief of the gang of grave robbers was Dr. Charles Morton, his brother. Police next arrested the doctor, together with a man named Thomas Beverly.    Morton immediately confessed.  His wife, who was with him, made an effort to save her husband, and offered to give the detective $100 for his release.  "I will not only give $100," she said, "but I will see that the bodies are returned inside

24 hours." The police declined the offer. She then vowed that she would shoot the man who had informed on her husband.

A search produced incriminating evidence at Dr. Morton's house. Among other tools, the police found a stained canvas sack, a rope, a shovel, and an augur bit. Several strong boxes filled with sawdust, which were evidently used for shipping bodies, were also discovered. Further investigation revealed that bodies had been shipped from the American Express office in Toledo to A. H. Jones & Co., Ann Arbor, Michigan

At the time of his arrest Dr. Morton claimed to be 35 years of age, and a graduate from the medical department of the University of Michigan. He said that he received $25 each for the bodies, and that poverty had driven him to adopt this macabre sideline. He and his gang had been in Toledo since about the beginning of 1878 and had been there for three weeks at the time of their capture. Morton remained in the custody of the police to await trial on January 23.

Evidence of the size of the Morton business arrived at the Toledo post office in the form of two letters. These letters, addressed to Charles O. Morton, were delivered to the doctor by the Postmaster in the presence of officers who wanted to use them as evidence in the case. As soon as Morton was handed the letters, he quickly threw them into an open fire, and placed his foot on them, hoping to destroy them. The officers acted quickly and the letters were saved, though badly scorched. Both letters were from a William J. Jones and

Co., Ann Arbor, Michigan.

One letter referred to the bodies of an old lady and a young boy, saying that the latter was too tender, and that Morton shouldn't send any more bodies younger than fourteen years old. Enclosed was a check for $90. The letter went on to advise Dr. Morton not to stay in the Toledo area much longer, but to go elsewhere to secure the 70 bodies that they had contracted for. There was also a reference to 60 bodies that had been sent by Morton and his gang while they were operating in Columbus.

Taking information from the letters, the police traced the location of the two stolen bodies to the University of Michigan. Authorities at the school turned over the bodies to the Toledo police.

On January 23, Dr. Maximilian Jungbluth, on a routine visit to the Toledo jail, visited Morton in his cell and discovered the prisoner's body was covered with an eruption which closely resembled smallpox. He called in Drs. James M. Waddell, Albert W. Fisher, and W. C. Craven for consultation; all of them declared the malady to be smallpox. Dr. Jungbluth opined that Dr. Morton would not live another 24 hours. Acting upon the representations of the physicians the chief of police ordered the prisoner removed to the pesthouse, with a police officer detailed to act as guard.

Morton remained at the pesthouse until June 29, when in some manner he succeeded in making his escape. It was suspected then, and later admitted by physicians, that someone furnished Morton with croton oil. Applying the oil to the skin causes it to erupt with blemishes that resemble small-pox sores. It is easy to assume that the croton oil was given to him by a party in need of the materials that his kind of business supplied.

A little over a month later Morton arrived in Cincinnati. He told his new landlord that he was a physician who intended to settle in Cincinnati. A young and handsome blonde woman was with him who was introduced to Meyer as Mrs. Morton. He also had two assistants with him. Morton would later be described in the newspapers thus: *"a small man, short in stature and rather slim, his eyes and hair are dark, and the usual expression on his face is rather pleasing. He is about thirty-five years of age and lithe as a cat. His dress was always clean and neat..."*

It was Morton's custom to leave the boarding house about 8 each evening and return around 4 in the morning. Once when Mrs. Meyer once asked Morton where he always spent his nights, he replied that he was passionately fond of fishing, and occupied himself with the sport during the night. Oddly enough, Morton's wife often accompanied him on his fishing expeditions, and sometimes dressed in male clothing.

Morton and his wife remained at the boarding house until the discovery of John Scott Harrison's body at the medical college. When that news broke they packed their trunks and left for the C. H. & D. Railroad Depot, saying that they had plans to travel to Canada.

Charles Morton wasn't heard from again for almost eleven years.

# Chapter Seventeen

*"Doctors can not be educated without (bodies),
and though all the physicians of the county be
locked up, the work of body-snatching will still be
practiced.* [67]
-<u>Cincinnati Daily Times</u> May 31, 1878

John and Carter Harrison, accompanied by the
Eaton brothers and Bernard Devin, were still looking for
the body of Augustus. They had been urged by
someone from the Medical College of Ohio that they
should focus their efforts at the Miami Medical College
of Cincinnati. [41] Since that was a rival college, they ignore
this advice and instead released a card to the press
stating the following:

*"An intimation, emanating, as we are informed, from someone connected with the Ohio Medical College, having been put forth privately, to the effect that a search for the body of our friend, Aug. Devin, would be more effectual if prosecuted within the precincts of the Miami Medical College, of this city, we deem it only just, especially in the present excited condition of the public opinion, to state that from the first the Officers and Professors of the latter institution have furnished us every facility for a thorough search, and have thrown no impediment in our way. And when this rumor was brought them day before yesterday, they came forthwith to proffer any further examination we might be pleased to make, which we thankfully declined, having full confidence in their expressions of sympathy and proffers of assistance. And if they seemed to us to express no words in condemnation of the course of the Ohio Medical College Professors, we have no doubt that it was in accordance with the accepted views of medial etiquette, which we failed to recognize in our treatment by most of the Professors of the Ohio Medical College."*

*C. B. Harrison*
*J. S. Harrison*

Detective Snelbaker was not so inclined to reject the rumor. Acting on information that the body of Devin had been hidden in the cellar of the Miami Medical

College, he obtained a search warrant on June 9th. Accompanied by a deputy and a reporter from the *Cincinnati Enquirer,* he visited the college in the middle of a heavy rainstorm. The janitor, Edward Seichrist, when informed of the nature of the business of his visitor's call, attempted to appear at ease, but did not succeed. After getting the keys for the different rooms, the janitor suggested that they start upstairs. Detective Snelbaker had another idea.

"I guess we'll examine the cellar first." he said.

"All right, sir." Seichrist replied, giving him an uneasy look.

Lighting a lamp, Seichrist started toward the cellar stairs through his private apartment.[42] As he did so, he stopped and hurriedly whispered to his wife, Ellan. Snelbaker, noticing this, told his deputy to remain upstairs and watch the family. A few moments later, Lizzie, the janitor's daughter, hurriedly wrote a note which she gave to her younger sister, Flora. As Flora set out to deliver the message, she was halted by Snelbaker's deputy.

"Where are you going?" asked the deputy.

"To visit Dr. Clendenin." she replied. Dr. William Clendenin was the Professor of Surgical Anatomy at the Miami Medical College. "He told us to send him a note if any detectives or officers came here."[43]

"If it's all the same to you," replied the deputy, "Detective Snelbaker directed me to request no one to go out until he came upstairs."

"Very well." replied the girl, returning to her room.

The janitor's wife came back in to where the deputy was and made a remark about the violence of the rainstorm. Then she said: "I hope you don't intend to arrest my husband."

"Madam," the deputy answered, "we are merely searching for the body of young Devin."

"Yes, I know that, but Mr. Wappenstein and another officer were up here last week and they said the same thing, and the next day my husband was subpoenaed before the Grand Jury."

"The officers had nothing to do with that. All of the janitors of the medical colleges were called in for anything that they might know."

She became agitated. "I wish we were out of this place, anyhow. My husband never did anything, but what he was directed to do by the Faculty, and if he gets into trouble they have a right to stand by him."

The deputy assured her that Snelbaker was merely after the body of Devin, which seemed to calm her.

"I pity his poor mother." she said. "Of course it makes no difference to him where his bones are. I shouldn't want any of my folk resurrected or dissected, and neither would anyone else, I suppose."

Detective Snelbaker and the janitor came up from the basement. The search had been fruitless.

"I know that his body was buried in that cellar last Thursday, and I have my doubts if it is not down there yet," said Snelbaker.

Seichrist forced a laugh. "Well, you saw all there was in the cellar."

"I don't think I did," said Snelbaker, "but I think I will before I sleep. Come, no, I don't care if you have forty bodies here, if you will turn up Devin's body I will make no further search, and I will give it to my friends and not tell them where I got it."

"I tell you it is not here." said Seichrist.

"Very well," said Snelbaker, "If it is I will find it if I have to dig up every foot of ground in that cellar."

"Well, if you are going to bring a party here to dig," begged the janitor, "please to get them to cover up their tools when they come here so the public won't suspect what they are about to do."

The detective promised to do so, then turned to leave.

He went outside where he talked to his deputy, then retraced his steps to where Seichrist stood. The detective took him to one side and said that he had information about the janitor that claimed that he knew much more than he was telling.

Frightened, Seichrist said, "Suppose I tell you that the body you are searching for is not here, but that I can put you on the track of it?"

"Very well," replied Snelbaker. "If you do, it will save you a heap of trouble, and may be the means of preventing you arrest."

"When did Devin die?" asked Seichrist.

They told him. The janitor then revealed to them that there were no male bodies in the institution, but that there was a female body buried in the cellar.

Seichrist said that ordinarily he let nothing come in

or go out of the institution without a written notice from Dr. Clendenin. However, around the beginning of March a resurrectionist by the name of Dr. Gabriel had come to him and told him that Clendenin had given him permission to use the cellar of the college to store 'stiffs' and to prepare them for shipment to Ann Arbor, Michigan. There they would be put into pickle for Michigan University's medical students use next winter. Believing him, Seichrist had let Gabriel use the cellar for that purpose. From the description given by Seichrist of the man he knew as Dr. Gabriel, it was soon clear that he and Charles Morton were the same person.

The way in which Morton and Seichrist had conducted their business was quite simple. The building was not being used for classes that time of year. Only the dispensary was open, with two physicians in the office for free consultation from 2 p.m. to 4 p.m. every day. When a body was secured, it was brought to the college and Seichrist hid it there until Morton could prepare it for shipment to Ann Arbor. According to Seichrist's confession, the shipping had been going on for about a month, the address on the box or barrel always being Quimby & Co. When the discovery of John Scott Harrison's body aroused public indignation Morton still had one body, that of a woman. Morton had become frightened and buried the body in a shallow grave in the cellar.

Snelbaker and the deputy left, but returned to the building soon after. The janitor led them to the cellar where they proceeded to dig up the body. It had been placed about two feet under the ground and encased in an old sack. The body was that of an old woman, thin and emaciated. It was so decayed that Detective Snelbaker could barely stand to look at it long enough to satisfy himself of its sex. As soon as he was sure that it was not Devin's body he had the janitor rebury it.

The discovery that their college had been used to ship bodies was quite a blow to the Miami Medical College faculty, who had bragged of their innocence following the discovery of Scott's body in their rival's building. They had let it be known that any resurrectionist who brought to the Miami College any corpse procured from anywhere but the public burying grounds of paupers would be handed over to the authorities for punishment. The janitor had strict orders to receive nothing at the college, nor to allow anything to go out, without a written order by Dr. Clendenin. So confident were they that there were no bodies in their building that when the Harrisons came to search for Devin's body, the faculty invited them to search every corner of the building and told them to ask for anything that might assist them. The courtesy with which the Miami faculty acted was attested by the high praise expressed in the card the Harrisons issued to the press.

When Scott Harrison's body had been discovered, Clendenin had gone through the building to see that there were no disagreeable signs left of last winter's dissection. He examined the vat, which was empty and overgrown with cobwebs. Clendenin had given a statement to the papers on May 31, 1878, some say with glee, that the Miami Medical College would "...not tolerate the robbing of rural graveyards or private cemeteries to obtain them. We have never been in favor of this, and would sooner close the college than be a party to such transactions."

Seichrist was later called before the Grand Jury to make a statement. The Grand Jury must have believed that the faculty did not know of his actions for they were never summoned. Dr. W. H. Mussey of the Miami College was later quoted as expressing his anger at the deception of the janitor. Shaking his head, he assured the public that the rest of the Faculty were as indignant as he, as all had taken the greatest pride in the way in which the business of their college had been conducted.

As for Seichrist, he remained in his position as the college's janitor for a number of years after the incident occurred, receiving no punishment from either the college or the public.

# Chapter Eighteen

*"Augustus Devin was a near relative by marriage
of Dr. J. H. Gilcrist..., one of the members of the
(Ann Arbor Medical) College Faculty. Truth is
indeed stranger than fiction."*
-<u>Cincinnati Enquirer</u> June 15, 1878

On June 10th Detective Thomas Snelbaker went to
the American Express Company in Cincinnati and
obtained a list of all the packages shipped to Quimby
and Co. Then, after conferring with the Harrisons, he
left for Ann Arbor, Michigan, with a Cincinnati Enquirer
reporter tagging along.

Ann Arbor was different from the established
metropolis of Cincinnati. A relative upstart, it didn't

really become a town of any importance until the state university was located there. After Michigan was admitted into the Union in 1837, one of the first acts of the State Legislature was to appropriate money to erect buildings and to establish a University. The Legislature agreed to locate the University of Michigan in Ann Arbor. The first building was erected in 1841, only 17 years after Ann Arbor became a city and by 1851 the first medical classes were being held.

The medical professors had a particular problem procuring cadavers. The city of Ann Arbor was young, and so was its residents During his inauguration as Chancellor of the University of Michigan in 1852 Harry Phillip Tappen told his audience that *"We who have just come to this State meet every day with the old settlers who are not yet old men."*

By 1878 a great quantity of 'material' was needed by the college as the number of medical students ran up to nearly 500 each session. Although bodies were being shipped to the University, the few residents of Ann Arbor that did die rarely remained in their graves. The *Cincinnati Enquirer* reported in 1878 that several years earlier the citizens of Ann Arbor had an occasion to remove a cemetery to make room for the growth of the town. They had found nearly every grave empty, *'not even the most oldest and honored citizens being spared.'*

The reporter accompanying Snelbaker wrote a horrifying eye witness account of what they found in Ann Arbor.

*"June 12 - The five o'clock train from Cincinnati tonight brought Colonel Snelbaker, of your city, who arrived in search of a large number of bodies which had been stolen from the Avondale Cemetery, and various other burying grounds in and about Cincinnati, during the last few months.*[44] *Colonel Snelbaker has, as your citizens know, been, since the Harrison horror, carefully searching for the body of young Devin, the robbery of whose grave caused the finding of Hon. John Scott Harrison's body in the Ohio Medical College. He has been quietly working the matter up, and has, in the course of his work, found that a large number of bodies from Avondale, and many other cemeteries in that vicinity have been stolen from their resting places, shipped here by express, and delivered to the College authorities here; and he brought with him a long list of documentary and other proofs showing that Morton, the famous ghoul, of whose work in Toledo last winter in furnishing subjects for dissection here you have had a full account, had been systematically working the graveyards in that vicinity, sparing neither rich nor poor, high nor low, robbing indiscriminately and sending the bodies to all points, but mostly to this place, as subjects for the Medical Department of the State University at this place.*

*"A large number, he finds, and among them the body of Augustus Devin's, have been taken*

from their graves by Morton and his confederates, carried to the Medical College there, and injected and prepared for shipment, and, after being boxed, taken to the American Express office and shipped to Quimby and Co., Ann Arbor.

"In regard to the body of Devin, he has, he tells me, proof positive that it was taken from the grave on the night of the 22nd of May last, carried to the Miami College, on Twelfth street, and, after being prepared, was shipped by express to Quimby and Co., of this place, on the 24th, arriving here on the 25th, being received and receipted for.

"Arriving here today, his first inquiry was for Quimby and Co., which name he found to be, as he supposed, entirely fictitious, being simply a blind by which the College receipted for by the officers or employees of the College. This being definitely settled, there no longer exists a doubt of the fact that Devin's body had been shipped here, and that it was now, unless it had been put away to avoid detection, in possession of the College, and with it, as shown by the express receipts and bills, a large number, perhaps twenty or more, of other bodies from your city.

"Having gained this point, he immediately, accompanied by your correspondent, proceeded to a thorough search of the College for these bodies, particularly that of Devin's, for which there has been such a thorough search.

*Obtaining the necessary documents, he obtained the assistance of Sheriff Case, and just as the sun was sinking behind the western hills, the descent was made upon the College.*[45]

*"The building, a great, gloomy old stone pile, situated on the outskirts of the town, was found nearly deserted, the school term having closed, and nobody but the janitor in charge. After some protestations on his part, which were quieted by the display of documentary authority, he led the way to the cellar under the building, where he admitted there were a few bodies which had recently sent in, and been put in pickle by himself.*

*"Negley*[46]*, the janitor, is in himself the most revolting specimen of humanity that could well be found, and is well chosen for his terrible work, which he had followed for a quarter of a century, and which he seems to take a fiendish delight. He is a short, stout German, about four feet ten in height, with a broad, squatty form, hands which seem still foul and clammy from their frequent contact with the dead in all stages of preservation and decomposition. Upon his broad, badger-like face, surrounded by a fringe of gray, played an expression of mingled stupidity, coarse brutality and cunning, which made him most repulsive in appearance. He has been for twenty-five years in this fiendish work, and seems in it to find his only enjoyment, his only solace for his lonely hours.*

*"He at first stoutly demurred, refusing to turn up the bodies; but, finding the Sheriff in no mood for trifling, quietly led the way to the door of the cellar. As it was opened a sickening stench, the odor of the dead, decomposing bodies, was emitted, stopping the party for an instant only, when the determined Snelbaker, urging them forward, descended to the cellar, accompanied by the Sheriff and your correspondent.*

*"There, ranged along the side walls, were three monstrous vats containing a large number of dead bodies floating in brine. Piled high above these were a number of empty coffins rudely broken open and rifled of their precious dead, while upon a rough table in the center of the room was a mixture of red paint and nitrate of silver, used for injecting the veins. A paint-mill on a table at the hand showed that large quantities of this mixture was prepared and used, and scattered about the room promiscuously were empty boxes and barrels and trunks and casks, in which the bodies had been shipped hither from Cincinnati and other points. Some of these, bodies having been removed, were now filled with collections of thigh bones, ribs, skulls and other fragments of human beings. From the great tanks wherein floated the dead came a sickening odor, which, while it nearly overpowered those unused to such an experience, seemed rather a pleasant perfume to the old Ghoul Negley, who with terrible*

grimaces and contortions of the body, as though in anticipation of the horrors he was about to display, advanced to his work.

"First he hurled from their places huge rocks which had been placed above to weigh down and keep in place the bodies. Then, with bare arms, and expression of fiendish satisfaction, he began reaching down into the vats in search of the bodies. As the weights were removed they floated to the surface and were seen to be closely packed in tierces in the vats, like so many slaughtered hogs packed for market.

"First next to the front was the body of a young and handsome woman of about twenty-eight, with long, golden hair, matted and discolored by the filthy brine into which the body had been rudely thrown. The face was one of great beauty, and though discolored by the process, still showed that it was the face of one who in life had known no want, and upon which the cares of life had left no trace. Alongside of it, naked as was the first, lay the body of a large negro, in an advanced state of decomposition, the black skin in large clots slipping from its place, and revealing the discolored flesh. As the body floated to the surface with that of the woman, the short, kinky wool was falling from the head and floating in the water, mingled with the golden tresses of the woman at his side.

"Next in order beyond and pressing against the

body of the negro was that of an old man, his feet encased in rough, filthy woolen socks, the body again naked, the eyes sunk deep in the sockets, the mouth opened and filled with the liquid in which it floated, the features distorted and discolored beyond recognition, the shaggy, gray whiskers cut close, and were loosening their hold and slipped from the face.

"As old Negley made a dive at the body, preparatory to hauling it out of the vat, aided by a stalwart student, whom he had pressed into service, the old man prepared to remove the bodies from the vat, in order that we might see whether or not those for whom we searched were there. Seizing the first roughly by the head and shoulders, his assistant grasping the feet, the body was lifted to the edge of the vat, and without a word of caution or a show of tenderness, or even the consideration a human would use toward a dead animal, it was tumbled rudely to the stone floor, the beautiful head which had been pillowed on some manly bosom striking hard upon the stone floor, the shapely limbs and well-rounded form thrown prone into the cellar filth and bones, and the golden, streaming hair sodden with the filth of the vat, falling as evil upon and over the body, hiding it and the face from its shame.

"Stepping next to the body to bring himself higher above the tub, he again plunged forward into the tub, bringing next the body of the negro, and throwing it to the floor with mingled oaths and ribald jokes and exclamations. Reaching again down, he drew up the body of a consumptive young man, a mere skeleton, the skin slipping from the arms and legs, the hands red and boney, the face discolored, and the hair falling in great masses from the well-formed skull. This dropped upon the floor.

"He followed with another and another, until within a few minutes there lay upon the filthy stone floor, mingled with the bones and fragments of the apartment, a pile of twenty ghastly corpses of all sizes and colors, and ages and conditions; the old, the young, the emaciated, the well-rounded figure, the shapen and misshapen, black and white, pauper and honored citizens alike in one promiscuous heap.

"Then he reached down again and seizing a half-sunken, ill shaped object, he dragged it to the surface, exposing the body of a beautiful woman of about thirty, the abdomen ripped open, the limbs twisted and disfigured, and the black, streaming hair floating in the water about the head. Drawing it from the water he threw it suddenly upon the heap of corpses, and as it struck, an infant of perhaps seven months fell from the womb. Snatching it up with a ghoulish leer and in expression beyond description, his assistant held it up to full view and with a heartless laugh asked if that was the one of which we were in search. For perhaps an hour longer this fiendish, sickening work went on until the vats were emptied and no less than forty naked corpses lay in heaps upon the floor, of all ages, sexes and nationalities, thrown promiscuously together, without the lest order or attempt at order, a sickening mass of human corruption. The skin slipping from the limbs and bodies where they had been roughly handle, the hair falling from the heads, or saturated with brine, dripping its filth upon the bodies below. The dead, distorted, meaningless faces looking out through the dim, ghastly lamplight in all forms and in all terrible positions of countenance on the fiends, who were disporting with their sacred flesh.

"Then the work of inspection began. Colonel Snelbaker carefully inspected all the bodies which bore resemblance to the dead for whom he sought, and succeeded, he thinks, in identifying several of them. Young Devin's body he has a very accurate description of and has found one which so closely corresponds with it that there seems to be little doubt, from the description, that it is the one long sought for. The peculiar marks, the scar upon the leg, the missing teeth, the peculiarity of the foot, all are plainly observable. The black hair and mustache, and with these and the expression of the face, although much distorted and discolored, that leads him to believe *that his search has been successful. At least he feels sure that he has found several, perhaps a dozen or twenty, of the bodies from Cincinnati or immediate vicinity. In regard to Devin's body, he, although feeling sure that it is here, is not yet sufficiently certain that the decomposed and disfigured mass found is the one wanted, and will await the arrival of the relatives of the deceased, who will perhaps be better able to decide.*

*"Of the other bodies he feels confident that several are already recognized, and it is probable very many others will be. Of the Faculty, we have not seen a single soul. Some of them are believed to have taken an active part in procuring these subjects abroad, even participating in the work themselves, and it is expected there will be some further interesting and very startling developments within a few days."*

The reporter had interviewed Nagele as he pulled the bodies out of the vat. Nagele could not understand the fuss being made over the way that he was handling the bodies.

"They can't feel, you know." Nagele said.

"Yes, but their friends can." replied the reporter.

"Yes, if they know it; but if they do, and come and ask for them, we give 'em up."

"How long have you worked at this?"

"Twenty-seven years, and," Nagele added with a chuckle, "I have got pretty use to them."

"Were you afraid of the work at first?" the reporter asked.

"Yes, very much, but I have got over that. I used to have to carry 'em all upstairs on my back. I just took 'em by the legs, you see, this way, taking then by the feet over my shoulders, so." Nagele said, demonstrating his technique to the reporter.

"But, this outrageous way of handling them, this is awful."

"Well, they can't feel."

The reporter discovered that part of Nagele's job was to preserve the bodies. This he did by severing the carotid artery and injecting a strong solution of arsenic of soda. If the body was to be preserved for any length of time, he repeated the process a few hours later. In a day or two he then injected a solution of beeswax, red paint and varnish into the arteries. The veins were not injected unless they were to be specially studied. In those cases the veins were injected with the beeswax and varnish solution, with blue paint added instead of red. On completing these procedures, he then put the body in one of three vats, each vat ten to twelve feet long, five feet wide, and about four feet deep. The 'pickle' solution they held was made of saltpeter and water. Nagele's final task was to weigh the bodies down with heavy stones to prevent them from floating to the top of the brine.

Snelbaker and company returned the next morning. The bodies still lay uncovered in heaps, just as they had been thrown there by Nagele the evening before. The red-lead injected in the arteries and the material used in the pickling vat had given the bodies a reddish tinge, almost life-like, while the hair, partially dried, aided in the illusion that the dead had somehow returned to life. The reporter watched as the bodies were replaced into the vats.

> *"The old fiend never seems in full enjoyment of his existence unless surrounded by the dead... The spectacle presented, as he stood in that darkened vault, that den of horrors, amid the stifling stench that arose from the putrefying bodies which lay thick on every side, his ghoul-like, clammy hands upon his broad ill-shapen hips, and a fiendish smile of satisfaction upon his evil countenance, was one of horror - one that can never be effaced from the memory. He had dressed himself especially for the occasion, in the rough suit in which he performs his sacrilegious work, a dark clayey-looking frock and pants suggestive of fresh made graves, and covered with great splotches of red, as if the bodies had bled afresh at his touch, or that their blood was rising against him in testimony of his many crimes against the dead."*

Meanwhile another, much more public, scene was taking place on the street. Dr. William Herdman, Professor of Practical And Pathological Anatomy, was searching for Sheriff Case that morning.[47] Having finally found him, Herdman had a few words with Case about Snelbaker's visit to the college. He had just recently discovered that the Sheriff had permitted Snelbaker to search the college, and he demanded to know why anyone had been let into the college without his consent. He denied that any bodies had been received from Cincinnati for a number of weeks, and consequently the body partially identified the night before could not be Devin's. Sheriff Case reminded the doctor that he had a general order from Herdman that permitted him to enter the college at all times, which he thought excluded the need to see Herdman in person.

Dr. Herdman, having no answer to this, eventually sulked away.

# Chapter Nineteen

*"Down among the dead men, way beneath the ground, safe in Nagely's pickling vat, there was Devin found."*
-Detroit <u>Evening News</u> June 19, 1878

Detective Snelbaker returned to Cincinnati June 13 with news of his findings in Ann Arbor.

"While the description of which I had of Devin's body would have warranted me bringing back the one I had found," said Snelbaker, "I did not care to take the responsibility of so doing until the relatives should decide for themselves."

"I am also confident that there are from a dozen to two dozen Cincinnati bodies in the tanks, and I feel confident that several or all of them will be identified. One of these is a woman of about fifty, with thin gray hair and strongly marked features. Another is that of a man of about forty, with one eye missing, dark hair and of about medium height. There are several others of which I have to refuse at the moment to speak of in detail."

On June 15, Bernard Devin and George Eaton traveled to Ann Arbor to identify Augustus Devin's body. They reached the city about 5 p.m., but were unable to proceed any further until nightfall, because of the absence of Sheriff Case, who had the search warrant. He was finally located around 8 p.m. The Sheriff was doubtful about going that late at night, stating that he and Professor Herdman had had a misunderstanding when the previous warrant was served. Sheriff Case was afraid that Herdman might resist the warrant, or make it impossible for them to examine the vats..

The young men were insistent, however, so they started out to the University. Herdman, hearing of their arrival at the college, sent word to Devin and Eaton to come to his house without Sheriff Case. When they arrived Herdman tried to persuade them to accompany him alone to the college. He assured them that no legal process would be necessary to examine the three bodies that Detective Snelbaker had indicated resembled Bernard's brother. Eaton and Devin insisted, however, stating that Sheriff Case was the only person in Ann Arbor who would be able to recognize the bodies which Snelbaker had identified, and so should be present on the occasion. Herdman demurred for some time, but finding the men determined, finally relented.

A group of five people went to the charnel house to view the bodies: Herdman, Devin, Eaton, Case and E. W. Miller, a reporter from the Cincinnati Commercial. At the University they were joined by two medical students, who showed the visitors to the basement. There was some difficulty with the gas lights, so lanterns had to be obtained to light the room.

The two students then donned rubber overcoats. Throwing several heavy stones from the top of one of the vats, they plunged their arms into the brine and drew out the body of a emaciated young man, which they placed upon a rude table in the middle of the room. His eyes were out of their sockets, his hair had fallen out, and his flesh was stripping from the bone. Devin and Eaton were told to look at the body, and say whether it was the one they searched for.

"Those look like Gus' shoulders," Devin replied, "and I see there is a scar on the right ankle, such as he had, and two of his teeth were decayed, where two are missing from this body. It looks a good deal like him, but I am not positive, and would like to see some others."

Eaton believed that the first body was indeed that of Augustus.

"Well," said Devin, "It looks a good deal like him, but I am not positive, and would like to see some others."

"The two students seized another body by the shoulders and brought it to the surface. Young Devin held a lantern to its face, and after an intent look, took a steel probe that was lying on the table and ran it up the nose of the corpse.

"This is Gus." Devin exclaimed. "Here is the little hole he had in the wall of his nose, and here are the decayed teeth; here the mustache, and here the scar on the leg. It's Gus, and I'll take my oath on it!'

Eaton made a careful examination and agreed that the body was that of Augustus Devin beyond a doubt.

The body was in a better state of preservation than could have been expected. The eyes were almost obliterated, and the head was completely bare, but the rest of the body, although extremely thin, was in very good condition.

"Don't you think, young gentlemen, you had better take another look at the body?" inquired Herdman, looking grimly on. "It's very easy to be mistaken in these cases."

"Well, I'm satisfied it's my brother," said Devin, "but if you will take it out of the vat I will look again."

The body was taken out and placed by the side of the other. Both Devin and Eaton examined it critically again and again agreed that it was the missing one.

"Better look at the third body." suggested Herdman.

Another body was raised in the tank. While Bernard examined the mouth, an upper set of false teeth dropped into his hand.

"That's not Gus," he said, turning away and handing the teeth to one of the students. "He didn't have any false teeth. I am positive that one there," indicating the second body, "is my brother."

This being settled, the other body was returned to the tank. The two students took it by the arms and legs and tried to swing it into the vat. On the first attempt they stumbled and the corpse fell upon its head with a sickening thud. They succeeded in their work the second time, then the cover was replaced and weighed down with great stones.

The ghoulish work over, the Sheriff and those with him left the institution about 10 p.m. Herdman required Devin and Eaton to sign an affidavit as to the identity of the body, and agreed to have the body in a suitable condition for shipment to North Bend the next morning.

# Chapter Twenty

*"If Morton is so bad, what is the standing of the men who realize double the money they pay him for his crimes?"*
-<u>Cincinnati Commercial</u> June 22, 1878

The following morning when Devin and Eaton went to pick up Augustus' body at the University, they were presented with a bill of services. Senior medical students Benjamin Logan Euans and Mark Stephenson Pascoe, together with Nagele, demanded $30, half of the amount was for soiled clothing. Devin refused to pay, saying that it was exorbitant. The students then refused to give up the body.

Devin and Eaton went to Dr. Herdman, who refused

to become involved, saying that he had nothing to do with it, and that the body was theirs as far as he was concerned. Devin and Eaton left, but not before vowing to return with a lawyer.[48] On hearing this some of the older faculty members went to Herdman and persuaded him to assume responsibility for paying the students. The students were informed that they would be paid, and the body was released.

Word circulated about how coldly the Professor had acted, and how he had tried to make the brother of the deceased pay for the body. To try and clear the matter Dr. Herdman released a letter to the press.

> *Ann Arbor June 18, 1878*
> *"The public have been favored with many sensational dispatches from this place concerning the search by Cincinnati parties for a dead body supposed to have been sent here. This body was taken from its grave at North Bend, Ohio on or after May 21st last, and, it is claimed, was traced to the Medical Department of our University. It is an invariable rule that when friends of deceased persons come here for the purpose of searching for and identifying their dead, no matter how unfounded their suspicions or unlikely their story, their feelings are respected, and they are accorded full liberty of investigation, without any obstruction or hindrance whatever on the part of the University authorities. In this instance this rule was not departed from in the slightest degree.*

"*On Wednesday evening, Policeman Snelbaker, of Cincinnati, arrived here, and, without consulting the University authorities, went to the medical building in company with the Sheriff and a reporter of one of the Cincinnati papers. They obtained admission to the building and to the 'dead room' by representing to the janitor that I had given them an order to him to admit them, and Snelbaker hired the janitor and a student to handle about fifty bodies for them, taking them out of the preservative fluid in which they were packed. Three which were thought to resemble, somewhat, the one they were in search of were selected from the number. The janitor was then ordered to let the bodies remain where they were until the friends should come from Cincinnati. I did not hear of these proceedings until the next afternoon, and then only by accident. To the search itself I had no objection whatever, but to the manner in which it was conducted, risking as it did, the loss of several thousand dollars of University property, for which I was responsible, I did object decidedly.*

"*On Friday evening the friends came to identify the body. I sent to the hotel for them and went with them to the Medical Building. One of the three bodies were shown to them, and the brother was confident that he identified it. He examined it carefully, and was reminded that there were three that were suspect, but he* expressed himself as satisfied and did not care to see any more, and it was only through my urgency that they consented to examine the rest. The next body that was shown him bore but little resemblance to the one they had seen, but they were equally sure it was the one, and finally decided to take it. I immediately turned it over to them, only requiring, in view of the uncertainty which they had shown, that they furnish me with an affidavit that they believed it to be the one they wanted. This they expressed themselves quite willing to do, and did so the next morning. I reminded them of the bill that Snelbaker had contracted with janitor and student for handling the fifty bodies. Thy acknowledged it, and said that they would pay it. They then engaged some of the students present to put this body in shape for shipment, and for this purpose I furnished them with a coffin. We then left the building.

"Later in the evening they returned to the building, found the body prepared for shipping, and inquired of the students the amount of their bill, and were told it would be $30, including what the janitor and student had done for Snelbaker. They agreed it was reasonable enough, and would be paid in the morning. Upon going for the body Saturday morning, in company with the Sheriff, they refused to pay the bill, and were told by the students that they could not have the body until they did. Here their troubles began, and all arose out of their refusal to pay a just bill, which they themselves and their agent had contracted, and to which they had a right.

"With the assistance of the Sheriff they circulated the report on the street-corners that I would not let them have the body of their relative, and that I demanded that they should pay for it, a false and unjust statement, but one that naturally aroused the indignation of those hearing it. Excitement ran high. Not a penny had been asked in return for the expense the University had incurred for securing this body, and it was freely given them at their request, in spite of the knowledge that I had that it was the body of one to whom they were entirely unknown. The arrangement between them and the students I felt that it was a matter with which I had nothing to do, and so stated to them.

"The street rumors reached the ears of some of the Faculty, and one of them, coming to me, urged me to quell the excitement at any cost. This I could see no way of doing, unless I should ignore the services which the young men had rendered, and for which I knew full well their charge was reasonable, or by offering to pay the bill myself. The latter course, for the sake of peace and harmony, I at once adopted, and thus the affair was settled. No member of the Faculty was in any manner responsible for the bill which the parties voluntarily incurred. Neither are they, *as far as I can see, in any way responsible for the sensation which resulted from refusal to pay the bill."*

Devin and Eaton were surprised by this and responded to the outrageous letter with one of their own.

*"To the Editor of the Commercial:*

*"In reply to Dr. Herdman's widely circulated statement, we emphatically deny that we promised to any person at any time thirty dollars for the preparation of the body of Augustus Devin for shipment. Mr. Pasco did agree to wash the body and place it in a coffin without charge. And his conduct throughout the whole affair was that of a perfect gentleman. We never expressed ourselves satisfied with the appearance of the first body, nor did we claim it as the one we sought. It is true that Dr. Herdman sent for us to the hotel, but he stated that 'his object was to persuade us to go to the college without any officer, our own or any other, and above all, the scoundrel Case,' meaning the Sheriff.*

*"We know nothing about Mr. Snelbaker's contracts, but feel assured that he will meet all his obligations. When we went for the body with the express wagon the students asked us if we had paid Dr. Herdman. Mr. Eaton asked them 'For what?' They said 'We have a bill for $30 for*

showing up the bodies.' Mr. Eaton answered, 'We will pay no such bill.' Euans, the Assistant Demonstrator of Anatomy, followed us all about town, repeatedly demanding payment, pleading that he was a poor medical student, or his associate was, that Sifton had ruined a suit of clothes; that the janitor was old, and one of the boys was lame.[50] As for himself, he had plenty of money, it was for the others he pleaded. When we asked him why they did not demand it in person, Euans had no answer to make. Dr. Herdman says, 'that is a false and unjust statement that he (Herdman) demanded payment for the money.

"The students asserted positively when we went for the body and the bill was presented, that it was Dr. Herdman's orders not to let the body go until the bill was paid. Then we went to Dr. Herdman's office down in town, and he said, 'Gentlemen, I left no such orders, but you must pay the students for their trouble." Dr. Herdman says that no member of the Faculty was in any way responsible for the confusion resulting from the demand of payment of money. Is not Euans, Assistant Demonstrator of Anatomy, a member of the Faculty? He is the individual who raised the breeze. Negley, the Janitor, called Euans the Assistant for Dr. Herdman. We hope this denial is sufficiently positive in particulars. In general we pronounce Dr. Herdman's statement a mass of *falsehoods."*

> *Bernard F. Devin*
> *George C. Eaton*

Printed in the paper that same day was an article listing eighty-eight names of people who swore that they were personally acquainted with Bernard Devin and George Eaton for years, and that they were known to be honorable and truthful gentlemen. It also stated that one thousand more persons were willing to testify to the truthfulness of the young men.

A final warning was issued at the end of the article; because of the threats made by the scientists of Ann Arbor, Augustus Devin's grave would be guarded by armed men nightly so that the body would never go back to Michigan.[51]

# Chapter Twenty-One

*"Devin and Eaton started home on Saturday... At the depot one of the medical students... offered to bet Devin $50 that the body he had taken off was not that of his brother. Devin paid no attention to the fellow, although he felt strongly inclined to give him a good "overhauling..."*
-<u>Ann Arbor Register</u> June 19, 1878

Because of the delay at the University, the body of Augustus was placed on a later train than had been planned, leaving Ann Arbor on 5 p.m. Saturday evening. This caused the group to miss a connection in Toledo which delayed them twenty-four hours.

It had been expected that the remains would reach

North Bend at 10 a.m. Sunday morning, and at that hour, notwithstanding threatening skies, over four hundred people were gathered to follow Devin's body to Congress Green for the second time. When the news reached them of the missed connection, it caused no little disappointment.

Augustus' body finally arrived in Cincinnati on the Cincinnati, Hamilton & Dayton Railroad at 8 o'clock a. m. on June 17. Though the rain kept many people home who would have liked to have shown their respect, there were still over one hundred and fifty people were at the station to meet the train. Estep, the undertaker, met the company with the same casket Devin had been buried in before. The remains were transferred from the box in which it had been shipped, to the coffin. Friends and family were then permitted to view the body.

The casket was carried into the freight room of the depot, where the remains were viewed and identified. A cloth covered the upper part of Augustus' head, from which the hair had fallen out. The eyes had sunken deep in their sockets, and decay had touched the features. From the eyes down, however, the face was well preserved and easily recognized. As each person passed the casket they added their testimony that the body was that of Augustus Devin.

The viewing was partially done for legal purposes. Dr. Herdman had stated that the body was not that of Augustus. To undermine any legal action Herdman might pursue, several of those who viewed the body signed a certificate stating that they knew, positively, that the body returned from Ann Arbor, Michigan was that of Augustus Devin. This was done in front of A. R. Lind, a Justice of the Peace for Miami Township.

The body was then transferred to the Plum Street Depot. At 9:30 the Lawrenceburg Accommodation, and the attending friends, left with it for North Bend.[52]

The number of mourners had grown visibly larger by the time the coffin arrived at Congress Green. Exactly four weeks to the day had passed since Devin's body had first been laid to rest. Before it was lowered into the ground, the casket was again opened at graveside and the remains were allowed to be viewed. Nearly a month after his death, Augustus was buried for the second time.

# Chapter Twenty-Two

*"The Grand Jury have spent much time in making a thorough, complete and searching investigation... in regard to the finding of the clothes and body of Hon. John Scott Harrison..., some thirty witnesses having been summoned before us in the above case."*[1]
-<u>Cincinnati Daily Enquirer</u> June 18, 1878

The same day that Augustus was being reburied the Grand Jury handed down their verdicts against A.quilla Marshall and Dr. Charles O. Morton. Marshall was charged with concealing and secreting the body of John Scott Harrison. Morton was also charged for concealing Harrison's body, as well as for removing Augustus

Devin's body from its grave.[53]

Marshall gave bond on June 19, before Judge Nicholas Longworth of the Court of Common Pleas, for his appearance for trial when his case was called. Marshall was accompanied by his lawyer, T. A. Logan, and Drs. Bartholow and Whittaker, his bondsmen before the Magistrate.

Lewis W. Irwin, the Prosecutor, read out loud the indictment against Marshall.

"The Grand Jurors of the County of Hamilton, in the name and authority of the State of Ohio present that J. Q. Marshall, on or about the 29th of May, 1878, at the County of Hamilton, with force and arms, unlawfully and maliciously did conceal and secret in a certain place, to-wit the building of the Ohio Medical College, located in Cincinnati, the body of one John Scott Harrison, deceased, which said body had been lately before, by some person to the jurors unknown, unlawfully and maliciously been taken and removed from its grave, in the Township of Miami, without lawful authority - he, the said J. Q. Marshall, at the time he concealed said body, well knowing it had been unlawfully and maliciously taken from its grave, as aforesaid, contrary to the statute in such case made and provided and against the peace and dignity of the State of Ohio.

"And the Grand Jurors further present J. Q. Marshall on or about the 29th of May, 1878, unlawfully and maliciously did conceal and secrete in a certain place, to-wit the building of the Ohio Medical College in Cincinnati, the body of one John Scott Harrison, which had lately before, by one Charles O. Morton, unlawfully and maliciously been taken from its grave without lawful authority - he, the said J. Q. Marshall, at the time he concealed said body, well knowing it had been unlawfully and maliciously taken from its grave."

"How does he plead?" asked Judge Longworth.

Logan smiled to himself. The indictment had been made out in the wrong name! "Mr. Marshall is not ready to plead to the indictment." answered Logan. "I have only read it over, and while I am of the opinion that there are defects in it, I have not determined whether I will have Mr. Marshall plead or demur to the indictment.

"As to the amount of bail, I hope the Court will take into consideration the ability of my client to give bail, and the character of the offense. I tried to impress upon the Magistrate the fact that the bail ought not to be excessive, but I did not succeed. I hope that the Court will fix the bail at a reasonable amount, so as not to prejudice the case against my client. I believe that if there were any public feeling or prejudices which induced the Justice to fix the bail in the amount he did, such feelings no longer exist."

Irwin spoke up. "I think that the bail ought to be fixed at at least one-half the amount at which it was fixed by the Magistrate."

Judge Longworth shook his head. "Excessive bail should not be required in any case, the object being merely to secure the attendance of a prisoner with certainty for trial. This case is to be tried just as all other cases are, and the bail proportioned to the nature of the offense and the ability of the party to give it, and the probability or improbability of his running away.

"The limit of punishment for which this prisoner is charged is a $1000 fine and six months imprisonment. I'm fixing the bail at double the amount of the fine which could be imposed if the prisoner is found guilty, namely $2000. This should certainly insure the attendance of the prisoner upon the trial and not be burdensome or excessive."

Drs. Bartholow and Whittaker were offered as sureties. Irwin waived the usual examination of the sureties and the bond was executed.

Logan stood up. "I ask the Court for an early hearing on this case."

Irwin stood. "I will set the case as early a day as possible, but I cannot say when at this time."

Court was adjourned.

The failure of the grand jury to indict any of the faculty angered Benjamin Harrison. Along with Joseph C. Devin of Mount Vernon, a cousin of Augustus Devin's father, Benjamin vowed to press suit against each of the Ohio Medical, Miami and Ann Arbor colleges for $10,000.

The first suit to was to be instituted against the Miami College in the name of Amanda B. Devin, Augustus' mother, and afterward a similar proceeding was planned against the University of Michigan. Benjamin retained the services of attorneys Aaron Fyfe Perry and Herbert Jenny to help with the case.[54] The plea was to be that consequential and exemplary damages could be claimed from the colleges both as a recompense to Mrs. Devin and a protection to society in the future. They hoped to show that Mrs. Devin had suffered great mental anguish, and had been put to much expense in recovering the remains of her son.

"In the present state of public feeling," Benjamin stated to the local press, "I have very little to fear of an adverse verdict. The damage has been fixed at a reasonable amount, with the expectation that the jury will recognize this, and that a verdict will be rendered for the full amount named."

In the suit against the Medical College of Ohio, the Harrison estate retained attorneys George Hoadly and Edgar M. Johnson.[55] As in the other cases, the amount asked for was to be $10,000. These suits were believed to be the first ever of this sort in Ohio.

# Chapter Twenty-Three

*"Colonel Snelbaker arrived here ( at Ann Arbor) tonight and in all probability there will be, tomorrow, one less dead body in the vaults of the Medical College of Michigan University."*
-Cincinnati Daily Enquirer June 30, 1878

Detective Snelbaker returned to Ann Arbor on June 24 and the next morning went to see Dr. Herdman. The purpose of his visit was to gather as much information as he could on Dr. Morton. Herdman denied knowing where Morton was. The Regents of the University were in session and Dr. Herdman invited Snelbaker to talk to them.

After some discussion the matter was put in the

hands of Regent E. C. Walker, of Detroit, who then had a short talk with Snelbaker.

"It is of my opinion that Dr. Herdman should offer his services freely and use his utmost endeavors to assist in the apprehension of the body-snatcher." said Snelbaker.

Walker disagreed. "Unfortunately, the Regents and Faculty are not justified in allying ourselves with a detective and assisting him in a somewhat equivocal manner in hunting up a man whom the officers might want."

"Well," retorted Snelbaker, "It seems that no assistance will be obtained from you. I had wanted to know whether I could rely on you to help out, but I can see that I'll get no aid here."

As he started to board the train back to Cincinnati he told a reporter : "I thought that my search might be brought to a more speedy conclusion if Herdman had assisted me, but as it is I am confident of getting Morton very soon. In fact, it is not entirely improbable that I might nail Morton on my way home!"

Snelbaker told of his plans to return to Ann Arbor in a few days. He had decided to make his headquarters there for a time. "I plan to bring parties here with a view to identify more of the bodies in the University. I am confident that there are eight or ten bodies there sent from Cincinnati and the vicinity. I am confident of a speedy identification of one of the bodies, and there are others that may well be identified." Snelbaker added that Dr. Herdman had just returned from a trip to

Indiana and hinted that perhaps he had gone there to talk to Morton.

The reporter then went to talk to Dr. Herdman and Professor Donald MacLean at the University.[56]

"Do you know where Morton is, Dr. Herdman?"

"I know nothing of the man's whereabouts." said Herdman.

"Have you received any letters from him since the grave robbery?"

Herdman waved the question away. "Morton procured the college bodies. The relation which existed between us was of a purely business character. Morton did not, and does not keep me informed of his whereabouts, and of course at the present time he would be very unlikely to inform me of his place of concealment."

"I think it is highly improbable that any one here at the college knows where Morton is." agreed Professor MacLean. "However, if any one here does know, and should disclose it, that act would call down upon the informer the general hatred of all body snatchers, which could prevent the University in the future from obtaining an adequate supply of material for anatomical purposes."

When Snelbaker returned to Cincinnati the following day he was met at the station by reporters, who started pumping him for 'something fresh.'

"Anything startling to tell, Colonel?" asked one.

"Well, I might give you some rather huge information, but just now it's policy for me not to do it. You see, it would defeat some of the things I am working for were I to allow these facts to go into print."

"Well, isn't there something you can tell that will not prejudice your work?"

"Well, probably; what do you want to know?"

"Did you identify any of the bodies?"

"Yes. I know who the golden-haired woman was."

"From Cincinnati?"

"No."

"Where then?"

"Michigan."

"Where did all those bodies come from, anyhow? Did you find out?"

"Yes. Thirty-two were shipped from Cincinnati to B. H. Stevenson and Company, Ann Arbor; two were from Logansport, Indiana, two from Erie, Pennsylvania, and from fifteen to twenty from Indianapolis."

"Who sent them?"

"Morton and his gang. Morton jumped from Toledo to Indianapolis and was working there during the latter part of last February and the first of March."

"You said Morton and his gang, I believe?"

"Yes. He has three confederates - two women and a man. His brother sometimes helps him."

"Do you expect to catch him?"

Snelbaker winked his eye and looked solemn.

"Know where he is?"

He winked the other eye. In evasion he said, "This Morton was shot once. When I was Chief of Police I arrested Henry Godar for stealing the body of a prominent Mason over in Newport. Morton was with him at the time and both were shot.  Morton escaped, but Godar was captured and convicted."

"When did this happen?"

"About two and a half years ago."

"Then you know Morton?"

"Yes."

"The work is not over yet?"

"Not by a gug full.  Good evening, gentlemen."

"Evening."

Snelbaker, "the successful and now famous detective", as one paper called him, could do no wrong. Unfortunately, his reputation as a master investigator was about to come to an abrupt end.

A couple of days after his return to Cincinnati, Snelbaker received a letter from a Dr. J. M. Bash of Warsaw, Indiana.  In the letter he stated that his brother, Jonathan, had died in Indianapolis and was buried in the nearby town of Allisonville on March 8.  Within days there was a rumor that his brother's grave had been robbed.  A friend of the family had investigated and found that the body had indeed been taken.  He informed no one of his discovery, thinking that it would do no good, since he believed the body  would be impossible to recover .  He informed the mother of the deceased that the rumors were false, and that her son remained in his grave.  It was only in the last week that Dr. Bash, residing a hundred miles away in Warsaw, learned of the fact and ascertained the truth.

Bash believed that his brother's body must have been stolen within a day or two of his burial.  The Indiana

Medical College, in Indianapolis, had not needed material at the time, which led him to conclude that the body of his brother was not there.

The letter contained a full description of the body, which Snelbaker believed to correspond with one he had seen in Ann Arbor. The detective telegraphed Dr. Bash to come to Cincinnati, which he did, arriving there Friday evening, June 28. They immediately left for Ann Arbor, arriving the next day on the afternoon train. A search warrant was obtained and by nightfall nearly fifty bodies were again in piles on the University's cellar floor.

After a careful inspection, they found a body that Snelbaker thought was the one they were searching for. Dr. Bash was not quite as certain. His brother had been taken from his grave nearly four months before, and had been stored in brine that entire time. The eyes of the corpse were gone, as was one half of the beard and mustache and much of the hair.

The next morning Snelbaker and Dr. Bash returned to the cellar. The body had been wrapped in a cloth and soaked in a solution of arsenic of soda to keep it preserved the night before. The solution seemed to bring out more clearly the features of the deceased. After looking at the body once again, Bash was convinced.

"That's my brother, there can be no doubt." he exclaimed.

The body was then taken to a local undertaker, who placed it in a common wooden box for reshipment. The box was filled with charcoal as a disinfectant.

The newspapers printed the story, telling their readers that even the relatives of the deceased were reading of the discovery of the body for the first time, since Dr. Bash had not wanted the family to know of his search until he was certain of finding his brother.

Snelbaker had reporters convinced that before the summer was over that half of the forty-odd bodies left at the University would be identified by him.

The next morning Detective Snelbaker left for Cincinnati on the 2 a.m. train. Bash stayed behind, electing to travel with his brother's remains to Indianapolis.

At 8 a.m. a dispatch arrived for the doctor and was delivered to the hotel where he had been staying. Learning that Dr. Bash had already gone to the train station, the telegram boy hurried to the depot, arriving just a few moments before the train was scheduled to come. The boy found Dr. Bash and handed him the message.

An express wagon came down with the remains a few minutes later. Bash told the driver that the body was not going to be taken after all. He said that he had received a telegram from Indianapolis stating that a mistake had been made- his brother's body was still in its grave. Bash told the expressman to see that the body was taken back to the University, and that he would see that all expenses were paid.

Just then the train pulled in. Dr. Bash entered one of the cars, and a few moments later was on his way home without the remains.

Dr. Herdman was informed of this unexpected phase in the case. He seemed to take great pleasure in the information. "I hope that the results of this will satisfy people of the difficulty of identifying a body and of the great uncertainty of the results. I knew all the time that the body which Dr. Bash wanted was not here for this reason; Dr. Bash's brother was buried on the 8th of March, and my records show that a body was received here from Indianapolis on the 9th. Bash was buried at Allisonville, twelve miles from Indianapolis, and it would have been a physical impossibility to have resurrected the remains and effected their arrival here in one day. Of course, while I knew all the time that the body was not that of the deceased, I knew further that there would be no use in denying the identity. In cases like this, persons visiting medical colleges are wont to be suspicious and doubt every word which is spoken to them by the authorities. They would have thought I was lying in whatever I would have said, so there was no good in saying anything. Whatever blame attaches itself to any one in the present case must belong to Dr. Bash himself, for it was he who employed Colonel Snelbaker to work up the case, and it was he, of course, upon whom the identity of the body chiefly rested.

"As for the golden-haired lady who still lies in the vault here, it never came from Cincinnati at all. It was received here in January, and no bodies were shipped from Cincinnati till four weeks or more later."

The misidentified body was sent back to the express office. Once there it seemed there was no one whose business it was to remove it. The undertaker had shipped it, but he did not want it returned to his rooms. The expressman did not want to carry it around anymore, and so it stood on the sidewalk in front of the Express Company's office most of the morning. It was finally taken back to the college later that day.

No mention was ever made of Snelbaker returning to Ann Arbor after the Bash affair. The awful incident seemed to make a point to others that the dead should be left alone, and that perhaps even Augustus Devin's body was not resting in its own grave after all. Yet in light of all the talk of different conspiracies between the doctors and the various colleges, it is somewhat of a surprise that none was mentioned between Dr. Bash and Dr. Herdman.

Consider this. Herdman returned from a trip to Indiana about the 25th of June. A day or so later Dr. Bash, *a doctor from Indiana*, asked Snelbaker's help to find a body. Coincidence? Perhaps the detective had become such an annoyance that the two doctors planned a way to make him look a fool, and to discourage him from setting up an office in Ann Arbor. If so, the plan worked. Dr. Herdman left on the same day that he received the news that Snelbaker had been wrong. This trip was supposed to be to Marietta, to visit his wife who was an invalid. Perhaps so. Or perhaps it was to Indiana to celebrate the success of a well-thought out plan beautifully succeeding.

# Chapter Twenty-Four

*"I expect I will have to go to Cincinnati sometime this month to try that case for the stealing of my father's body. You know how I dread to go over the details of that horror again - but I don't see how it can be avoided."*
-Benjamin Harrison in a letter to Margaret Peltz
October 11, 1878


No records have been found indicating that Aquilla Marshall went to trial or that any civil suits were filed against the colleges. Perhaps the several mistakes made in the warrants used to arrest Marshall and search the colleges, and Benjamin Harrison's unwillingness to discuss the stealing of his father's body, made it seem unwise to pursue the matter.

Marshall continued on as janitor for the Medical College of Ohio until his death three years later, when the position was given to his wife Mary.

On June 18, 1878 John Harrison, on behalf of the family, presented Constable Lacy with a handsome ebony cane, as a testimonial of the family's gratitude. Lacy was "too much overcome with emotion" to reply, but the hearty handshake of the Harrison brothers showed that no words were necessary. The cane bore a silver plate inscribed: "Presented to Walter Lacy, by the sons of John Scott Harrison, May 30th, 1878", the date they found their father's body.

On June 24, 1878 Bernard Devin received an anonymous letter threatening *"to have (Augustus') body at all hazards."* Devin's body was then moved to a vault in Greendale, Indiana. It is believed Augustus' body was later returned to Congress Green, although no records of this have been found.

The Medical College of Ohio prospered from the publicity. Their 58th Annual Catalogue and Announcement for 1878-79 reported that arrangements had been made for a dissecting class of 300 students, 100 more than the previous year. Dr. William Seely became Dean of the College in 1881, staying in that position until his retirement in 1900.

John Scott Harrison's body was later returned to Congress Green on December 13, 1879, where it was placed in the family vault. This occurred with little publicity.

In 1881 a new anatomy law was passed, which increased penalties against resurrectionists, but also provided more ways to legally obtain bodies.[57] The fine for the unlawful possession of a dead body was increased from one thousand to five thousand dollars and a jail sentence of six months in the county jail became imprisonment in the much harsher penitentiary for a period of one to five years.

In February, 1889, Benjamin Harrison, the newly elected President of the United States, learned some startling facts about the man who had stolen his father's body.

Charles Morton, alias Dr. Gabriel was, in fact, an Englishman named Thomas Miller Beach.

Thomas' parents were John and Maria Beach. Born in Colchester, Essex on September 26, 1841, he was the second son of what was to become thirteen children. Hearing of the outbreak of the American Civil War, he traveled to America to fight for the north.

Thomas Beach took on the name of Henri Le Caron on August 7, 1861, the day he enlisted in the 8th Pennsylvania Reserves as a private. He later transferred to the Anderson Calvary. It was during the war that he met his wife, Nannie.

On demobilization in February 1866 Le Caron joined the veteran organization of the Army of the Cumberland and the Grand Army of the Republic, being listed as major. He chose to be known by this rank from then on.

About this time, Le Caron became interested in the

Fenian Brotherhood, an organization of Irish-Americans, who sought to win the independence of Ireland from Great Britain. After an unsuccessful attempt to emancipate Ireland failed in 1865, the Senate Wing of the Fenian Brotherhood was formed in the United States. Their plan was to invade the British-held land of Canada, which could then be used in negotiating Ireland's freedom. Le Caron was told of this plan by John O'Neill, a man he had become friends with during the Civil War. Upset, he wrote his father in England. His father wrote back, saying that he had handed over Le Caron's letter to the government, and that the House Secretary was interested in any details of the upcoming invasion that could be found. Le Caron reported back to his father whenever he acquired new information. The raid into Canada took place June 1, 1866. It was a dismal failure for the Fenians.

Le Caron returned to England in 1867. He was approached by the English government and asked if he would agree to become a paid British agent, return to America, and infiltrate the Fenian organization. He agreed to do so.

Le Caron would later be described by the *Daily Graphic* newspaper as *"Perhaps the most daring spy that ever lived."* He kept the Canadian government informed of Irish-American preparations for yet another armed invasion into Canada in 1870 and warned Scotland Yard of an Irish bombing campaign in England.

Why would a man who worked for the British government become involved in body snatching? An explanation can be found in the introduction of Le Caron's autobiography, *"Twenty-five Years In The Secret Service: The Recollections of a Spy"*.

> *"There is a popular fiction, I know, which associates with my work fabulous payments and frequent rewards. Would that it had been so. Then would the play of memory be all the sweeter for me. But, alas! the facts were all the other way... in the Secret Service of England there is ever present danger, and constantly recurring difficulty, but of recompense, a particularly scant supply."*

Henri Le Caron first began robbing graves in 1872 to support himself through classes at the Detroit Medical College. At first he limited himself to the state of Michigan, but he soon branched out to Indiana and Ohio. His name naturally suggested to those who knew him the title of 'Carrion", which was very appropriate for his business. A favorite field of his was the Catholic cemetery in the rear of the town of Sandwich, just across the river in Canada. The country graveyards in the vicinity of Ann Arbor were also the objects of his earnest attention.

In 1889 he was asked to testify in England of his involvement with the Fenian organization in America. Under the headline *"Le Caron - The English Spy's Career in Michigan Now Laid Bare. Resurrected the Body of President Harrison's Father"*, the *Detroit*

*Evening Journal* told of Henri Le Caron's involvement in John Scott Harrison's resurrection.

Le Caron's testimony was a great blow to the Fenian cause. The New York *Herald* interviewed Le Caron on how the testimony had put his life in jeopardy.

> *"As to the danger in the future, I am prepared for anything that may happen. I have done what I thought right to do and I will bear the consequences. Where I shall go and what measures I shall take to protect myself against assassins is a subject on which I have the best reason in the world for keeping silent. It is needless, however, for me to say that I shall not settle in Chicago, nor shall I make a visit to Ireland.*

Le Caron went into hiding. His face had become well known from the pictures that had appeared in numerous newspapers and magazines. It was no secret that many Fenian sympathizers wouldn't have minded seeing him dead. Le Caron lived in suburban hotels outside London for some time, being watched over by detectives. His wife and children lived in a separate dwelling in Brixton so that they would not be recognized as being associated with him.

Eventually the family was reunited. Le Caron's memoirs of his time as an English spy was published in 1892. The book was a tremendous success and was reprinted as late as 1974.

Henri Le Caron passed away on April 1, 1894. Fenians in Britain and America were not convinced. They believed that his death had been falsified to deceive any would-be assassins. Ralph Meeker, the London representative of the New York *Herald*, obtained permission to see the body and he reported that Le Caron was indeed dead.

Le Caron was buried at Norwood Cemetery on April 7th. A four-foot marble cross was chosen as his head stone. Upon it was inscribed *"IN LOVING MEMORY OF HENRI LE CARON. DIED APRIL 1ST 1894. AGED 51. THY WILL BE DONE".*

The cross now lies fallen on the ground, the man buried there all but forgotten.

# FOOTNOTES

1  When John Scott Harrison's father William was asked to become Minister of Columbia, he accepted.  Although John Scott was working at the law firm of Longworth and Harrison at the time, he felt compelled to come home and manage the farm, something he had learned early on as a boy since his father's various official duties included having to travel for long periods of time.

To show his gratitude, John Scott's father gave him almost 400 acres of land and built him a sturdy brick home in 1837, which came to be known as Point Farm.

2 Morton served as Governor of Indiana from 1861 to 1867, and from there turned to the United States Senate.  His death opened the way for Benjamin Harrison to become the State Republican leader.

3 John Scott Harrison was a member of Congress for the First Ohio District from 1853 to 1857.

4 Augustus was the son of William B. and Amanda Devin. William was the brother of Thomas Devin, who was married to John Scott Harrison's daughter, Sarah.  Augustus had been buried on May 21, 1878.  He was 23 years old at the time of his death.

5 The last words he had penned were *"The value of a Christian mother's work within the precincts of our own houses will never be properly estimated until that day when..."* Here the sentence ends.

6 It was on July 5, 1831, the result of a conversation at a 4th of July celebration that William and Anna Harrison donated the property on which the church was built. The ground was deeded to the trustees of the church, Stephen Wood, Daniel G. Howell and Andrew Porter, for $1. The original deed is located in the Presbyterian history section at the University of Cincinnati Library.

   Although donating the ground, William never became a member of the Cleves church. He did, however, attend services and taught a Sunday school class.

7 The other pallbearers were James J. Faran, Robert Brown, John Whitman, Ebenezer Argo, Robert Hodge and Philander Gillespie.

8 The Presbyterian Church at Cleves was founded by Horace Bushnell, who went to Cleves expressly for that purpose. Because he was an Abolitionist he was refused any place to board. Seeking out a deserted cottage, he plastered it with mud and moved in. Through his persistent efforts the church was organized in 1830. The building was erected a year later, then added onto in 1850. Bushnell was a pastor in the area for over half a century, until his death at the age of 81.

9 Congress Green was located on a hill just west of North Bend. Located on "the mound" was the Harrison family vault, where laid the remains of William Henry Harrison, his wife

Anna, and one of their daughters. Near the center of the inclosure proper was the Harrison lot, containing the graves of the descendants of William Henry Harrison and also those of Anna Harrison's father, John Cleves Symmes, founder of North Bend. The inclosure was fenced in at the time. Augustus Devin's grave was located just outside the fence line on the east side of the inclosure.

10 He left behind six children. They were Benjamin Harrison, of Indianapolis, Indiana; Mrs. S. V. Morris, of Indianapolis, Indiana; Mrs. Elizabeth Eaton (married to Dr. George C. Eaton); Mrs. Sarah L. Devin (married to Thomas Devin), of Ottumwa, Iowa; John H. Harrison, of Kansas City, Kansas; and Carter Harrison, of Point Farm, Ohio.

11 Census records of the time period show a number of stone masons, stone breakers and stone workers in Miami township. Many were undoubtedly engaged in bridge building along the Miami and Whitewater Rivers.

Railroad companies were constantly having to rebuild their bridges. Frequent flooding in the valleys stirred up the river beds of gravel and washed out bridge supports.

12 One source claimed the stone was so large that it's *"weight required the united strength of 16 men to overcome."*

13 Augustus' father, William, had died on January 2, 1866 at the age of 42, after being scalded during an explosion that occurred at the sugar factory where he worked.

14 The Medical College of Ohio was often referred to as the Ohio Medical College.

15 Snelbaker had once held the office of Superintendent of Police of Cincinnati from Feb. 1875, until he was succeeded by Captain Jacob Johnson in 1877.

16 The Medical College of Ohio was incorporated on January 19, 1819 and organized a year later. It was the second medical school established west of the Allegheny Mountains, the Transylvania school in Lexington, Kentucky having started three years earlier. The building on Vine and Race streets was erected in 1851.

The Medical College of Ohio and the Harrison family had several connections. William Henry Harrison had studied medicine and his interest in the subject continued all of his life. He served on the board of the Medical College of Ohio in 1822.

William H. Harrison's daughter, Lucy, was the wife of David K. Este, who was a member of the first board of trustees of the college.

17 This was not unusual. Many times the faces of the subjects brought into the colleges were slashed to make identification more difficult for anyone who might come searching for a loved one. Stolen bodies were purposely disfigured to avoid detection. A solution of nitrate of silver changed the skin color. Another method was to skin the face. If a scar or other distinguished mark was found, this would be mutilated and disfigured beyond recognition.

18 A graduate of Yale in 1862, he studied medicine at the Medical College of Ohio and completed his medical studies in Vienna. In 1865 the chair of ophthalmology and otology was created and Seely was appointed to fill the position.

19 Dr. Frederick C. Waite based his estimate on his statistical study of physicians. This was told to Linden F. Edwards in a personal letter to him by Waite. Edwards told of this in his article <u>Body Snatching in Ohio during the Nineteenth Century</u>.

20 <u>Daniel Drake And His Followers</u> by Otto Juettner

21 The reason that the fire department knew of the discovery of John Scott Harrison's body was never explained, but since the headquarters was located next door to the college, it seems likely that George Eaton stopped there to ask for the location of the nearest undertaker.

22 Allan Pinkerton founded the Pinkerton National Detective Agency in 1850 to investigate cases of freight theft on the railroads. He aided the Union during the Civil War, heading an organization engaged in spying on the Confederacy. Pinkerton made a name for himself when he uncovered a plot to assassinate President Abraham Lincoln in 1860, which he foiled through quick and precise planning.

23 <u>Daniel Drake And His Followers</u> by Otto Juettner

24 Jacob Strader was part owner of Harkness, Strader and Fosdick, a cotton factory.

25 The county jail was located on the west side of Sycamore Street, at the rear of the courthouse.

26 Phineas Sanborn Conner was Professor of Surgical Anatomy. Frederick Forchheimer was Professor of Medical

Chemistry and Demonstrator of Morbid and Physiological Histology.

27 Marshall had a wife, (Mary, age 33), four daughter, (9 year old Mary, 4 year old Lillie, 2 year old Josie, 1 year old Nannie), and a son (William, age 4). The family had living quarters in the Medical College of Ohio building.

28 The bonds read as follows:

*State of Ohio, Hamilton County. Before me, B. M. Wright, a Justice of the Peace in and for Cincinnati Township, of said county. The undersigned, James T. Whittaker, a resident of Hamilton County Ohio, proposed surety on the bail bond in the above stated case, being duly sworn, says that he is worth, when all his debts are paid, at least $10,000, and that he has property liable to execution in the State of Ohio, amounting in actual value at least to the sum of $10,000, beyond the amount of all his debts and liabilities.*

*James T. Whittaker*
*Sworn to and subscribed in my presence, this 31st day of May, 1878.*

*B. M. Wright*
*Justice of the Peace*

*The State of Ohio, Hamilton County, ss.*
*Be it remembered, that on the 31st day of may, in the year 1878, A. Q. Marshall and James T. Whittaker personally appeared before the undersigned, a Justice of the Peace in and for the county aforesaid, and*

*severally acknowledged themselves to owe the State of Ohio in the sum of $5,000 to be levied on their goods and chattels, lands and tenements, if default be made in the condition following, to-wit:*

*The condition of this recognizance is such, that if the above bound A. Q. Marshall shall personally be and appear before me, at my office, in the township of Cincinnati, in the said county, at 8:30 o'clock a.m., on the 6th day of June, in the year aforesaid, then and there to answer to a charge of receiving, concealing and secreting a certain dead body, and abide in the judgment of the Court, and not depart without leave, then this recognizance shall be void, otherwise it shall be and remain in full force and virtue in law.*

*A. Q. Marshall*
*James T. Whittaker*

*Taken and subscribed before me, the day and date first aforesaid.*

*B. M. Wright*
*Justice of the Peace*

29 Marmaduke Burr Wright joined the Medical College of Ohio in 1838 as Professor of Materia Medica and Therapeutics. He resigned in 1868, but was an emeritus Professor of Obstetrics in 1878, as well as a member of the board.

30 Seely's remark on the finding of John Scott Harrison's body, that "it will all be the same on the day of resurrection", led many of the public to believe that Seely took the matter of John Scott's body being stolen quite lightly.

31 For all of his supposed indignation, Dr. Wright was no stranger when it came to body snatching. In his book <u>Daniel Drake and His Followers</u> the author Otto Juettner reprints a story that Wright would tell his students when recalling the good old days.

*"I was one of four who had agreed to exhume the body of a man of immense size. After procuring the necessary pick and spades, rope and sack, we proceeded to the designated place of burial. But the light from the surrounding windows fell brightly upon the tomb-stones, and rendered it unsafe, at so early an hour, to engage in the execution of our task. Wrapped in our cloaks, we lay concealed in the dark shadows of the church until after midnight. Then we assumed the duties assigned us. One was stationed at the entrance, another at the outlet of the graveyard, as sentinels, while a third and myself commenced the digging. No countersign was given of approaching danger, until we had reached the lid of the coffin. It was made of thick boards, and fastened with long screws, so that much force was required to break it. It gave way with a loud noise, which resounded from house to house, and roused the faithful watch-dogs from their slumbers. A general barking ensued, lamps were lighted, and forms were dimly seen, passing the windows. Not a footstep, however, was heard approaching us, and we returned to our labor, which had been temporarily suspended. A rope was fastened around the neck of the corpse, and , after much and long continued effort, it was dragged from it's resting place. We had not gone far with our burden, when, as we turned a corner, a man*

*came suddenly upon us. We did not falter, for we discovered at once that he was a staggering drunkard. At length we became weary, and transferred our load to a wheelbarrow, which we found after much search under a woodshed. It gave relief to our shoulders, but the noise of its rusty axle grated harshly upon our ears. Daylight was fast approaching, smoke was issuing from many a chimney, the butcher's wagon was passing on its way to market, and every step we took was attended with hazard. In sight of home we came to a halt. 'Doctors, what have you got there?' inquired one gruffly. With our hearts in our throats, we fell back a short distance, and watched the movement of the intruder. We saw him lift the sack, and place his hand upon its cold, human contents - we saw him start - shudder- and, with uplifted hands, run out of sight. We seized this as the only favorable moment of escape, and carrying our treasure with us, reached the place which had been prepared for our reception."*

32 His predecessor had been discharged for carelessness and inefficiency.

33 John Kelly, a grave digger employed by Spring Grove since 1857, was later interviewed by the <u>Cincinnati Commercial</u>. He claimed that he had never known of a single instance where a body had ever been found missing from its grave where it was interred, even though he had assisted in removing many bodies from one grave to another within the cemetery. And, although many resurrections have been listed in the Cincinnati papers over the years, the author has never found one connected to Spring Grove Cemetery.

34 For years many citizens had asked that the cemetery be removed to another location. Over 25,000 bodies lay on an elevation above the common level of the village. The drainage of the cemetery on the slope next to the Pike naturally found its way into adjoining wells, cesspools and deep cellars, which rendered nearby homes unpleasant and unhealthy.

35 Benjamin Harrison would later state that the loveliness of the place alone was monument enough for his grandfather because he had especially favored the view of the Ohio river.

36 The following letter was received by Benjamin Harrison the next day:

> *Hon. Ben. Harrison, Brothers, Sisters and Friends:*
> *The managers of Greendale Cemetery extend to you their heartfelt sympathy in the terrible calamity which has befallen you, and suggest to you the propriety of reinterring your father and family at Greendale Cemetery, and proffer you, free of expense, any plot of ground you may select for the purpose.*
> *The bearer, Dr. Robbins, will explain further to you. Sincerely yours,*
>> *Resin Rees*
>> *Wm. Probasco*
>> *Sam'l Dickinson*
>> *J. F. Vaughan*
>> *M. H. Hardigg*
>> *Managers of Greendale Cemetery*

37 For many years there was a standing offer by the officials of the Spring Grove Cemetery to the Harrisons of a lot in the

cemetery for the remains of William H. Harrison and his family. The idea of the removal of the remains was, however, somewhat distasteful to his widow, who desired not only that the ashes of the President should remain at the family cemetery in North Bend, but that her own should be laid beside them.

In the fall of 1879 Carter and Benjamin had the tomb repaired. The arched roof, which was sodded on top, was replaced with a flat roof, and the brick work covered with a thick cement coating set in squares.

In 1896 residents of Cleves and North Bend raised $1000 to repair the old tomb. The hillside was excavated, the burial space enlarged to hold 16 crypts and the entrance to the tomb was changed from the west to the south side. It was completed in 1897. A sixty foot monument in memory of William Henry Harrison was finally erected over the tomb in 1924.

38 The warrant read as follows:

*The State of Ohio, Hamilton County, ss:*

*Before the undersigned, a justice of the peace, in and for said county, personally came Bernard F. Devin, who being duly sworn according to law, deposeth and saith that at the county aforesaid, within ninety days past, the following to-wit: The body of S. Augustus Devin, has been by some person or persons feloniously taken or stolen and carried away from the North Bend burying ground, and that the body, or some part therefore, is concealed in the Ohio Medical College, of the township of Cincinnati, in the county aforesaid.*

*These are, therefore, to command you in the name of the State of Ohio, with the necessary and proper assistance, to enter in the day time or night time, into rooms of the said Ohio Medical College, of the township and county aforesaid, and there diligently search for the said body, and if the same, or any part thereof, be found upon such search, that you bring the body so found, and, also, the body of any person in whose possession and control said body may be found, before me or some other justice of the peace for said county, to be disposed of and dealt with according to the law.*

*Vincent Schwab*

39 Although Harry Cooper made his home in Cleves, Ohio, his law office was in Cincinnati.

40 Benjamin Harrison was a General during the Civil War.

41 The Miami Medical College was organized in 1852. In 1857 the college merged with the Medical College of Ohio. In 1860 the consolidation was broken up and the faculty reorganized. In the autumn of 1866 the Miami Medical College erected a building on Twelfth Street between Elm and Plum streets.

42 In 1878 Edward Seichrist was 44 years old; his wife Ellan, 40, daughter, Lizzie, 18; son Edward C., 15; daughter Flora, 13; son Selmar, 8; daughter Laura, 1.

43 William Clendenin was a graduate of the Medical College of Ohio in 1850. In 1856 he filled the position of

Demonstrator of Anatomy at Miami Medical College. After fighting in the Civil War he was appointed by President Andrew Johnson as Consul to Russia, which Clendenin refused. He returned to Miami Medical College in 1866, filling the chair of Professor of Surgical Anatomy.

44 Thomas Snelbaker was a Colonel during the Civil War.

45 The four-story Medical College, built in 1851 and expanded in 1865, was plastered with cement on the outside and checked in imitation stone-work. The body of the building was painted a light brown color, the cornice and trimming were a darker shade. On the third floor was the amphitheater where the students listened to their professor explain the various parts of the human anatomy while he dissected a body.

46 Gregor Nagele was the correct name of the janitor. Because of its pronunciation, Nagele's name was misspelled by the newspapers covering the story. Census records indicate that Nagele was 57 years old in 1878.

47 William James Herdman's first love was astronomy and geology. He had decided to make geology his life's work, when he was involved in an accident which required surgery. The study of his own case so interested him that he decided to study medicine, graduating from the University of Michigan in 1875. He then became a Professor of Practical and Pathological Anatomy and Demonstrator of Anatomy for the University of Michigan.

48 Devin had telegraphed his cousin, Joseph C. Devin, for the

money to pay the students. A postal amount was forwarded to Ann Arbor, but the faculty had by then informed Devin of their decision that they owed nothing to the students, and that the body would be released to them without further legal action.

49 In the <u>Cincinnati Daily Gazette</u> on June 18, 1878 an explanation was printed, telling the position of the Ann Arbor College. In part it stated that : *"The faculty of the (Ann Arbor) university wish to have it understood that no hindrances will ever be thrown in the way of anybody who thinks the bodies of friends are here. The brother of the dead man expresses himself entirely satisfied with his treatment here, except the charges for services rendered, with which the university, as such, not any of its officers, had anything to do."*

50 Alfred William Sifton was a medical student who graduated from the University of Michigan in 1880.

51 After the robbery of John Scott Harrison's body the citizens of North Bend and Cleves quietly organized themselves into a very efficient guard of Congress Green. With but one avenue leading down from the hill and only two roads from North Bend to Cincinnati, the roads were so closely watched that it wasn't possible for a buggy to pass without it having to undergo a careful inspection. People late in getting home at night were halted by the self-appointed sentinels and only allowed to pass if they had a good explanation for traveling so late.

52 The Plum Street Depot was a passenger depot located at the corner of Plum and Pearl streets. This depot was for the

Indianapolis, Cincinnati and Lafayette Railroad.

53   The two indictments against Charles O. Morton are as
follows:

> *1) The Grand Jurors of the County of Hamilton, in the
> name and by the authority of the State of Ohio, upon
> their oaths and affirmations, present that Chas. O.
> Morton, on or about the 29th of May, 1878, with force
> and arms, at the Township of Miami, in said County,
> without lawful authority, the body of one John Scott
> Harrison, deceased, from its grave there situate, in
> which it had then lately before been interred, and then
> was, did willfully remove and carry it away, contrary to
> the statute in such case made and provided, and
> against the peace and dignity of the State of Ohio.*
>
> *And the Grand Jurors further present that Charles
> O. Morton on the 29th of May, 1878, did willfully
> conceal and secrete in a certain place, to-wit: the
> building of the Ohio Medical College in Cincinnati,
> the body of one John Scott Harrison, which body had
> then lately before, by some person to the jurors
> unknown, willfully and maliciously been taken and
> removed from its grave without lawful authority, the
> said Morton, at the time he concealed the body, well
> knowing that the same had been removed as aforesaid.*
>
> *And the Grand Jurors do further present that said
> Morton, on the 29th of May, 1878, unlawfully and
> maliciously concealed and secreted in the Ohio
> Medical College, the body of one John Scott Harrison,
> which had been lately before by Charles O. Morton
> unlawfully and maliciously been taken and removed*

from its grave, and said Morton at the time he concealed the body well knowing the same to have been removed from its grave, contrary to the form of the statute in such cases made and provided, and against the peace and dignity of the State of Ohio.

2) The Grand Jurors of the County of Hamilton, upon their oaths and affirmations, present that Charles O. Morton, on or about the 29th of May, 1878, at the Township of Miami, without lawful authority, the body of one August Devin, from its grave, in which it had lately before been interred, did willfully remove, take and carry away, and the Grand Jurors present that on said day Charles O. Morton unlawfully and maliciously did conceal and secrete in a certain place, to-wit: the Miami Medical College in Cincinnati, the body of one August Devin, which said body had lately before, by some person to the jurors unknown, been taken from its grave without lawful authority - he, the said Charles O. Morton, at the time he concealed said body, well knowing it had been unlawfully and maliciously taken and removed from its grave.

54 One of Aaron Fyfe Perry's daughters, Edith, was married to Dr. Frederick Forchheimer of the Medical College of Ohio.

55 George Hoadly would later serve as the Governor of Ohio from 1883 to 1885.

56 Dr. Donald MacLean was Professor of Surgery for the University of Michigan.

57 (Paraphrasing:) "All superintendents of city hospitals, city and county infirmaries, workhouses, asylums for the insane, or other charitable institutions supported in part by public expense, or wardens of the penitentiary, sheriffs or coroners in possession of bodies not claimed or identified, or which must be buried at the expense of the county or township shall, on the written application of the professor of anatomy of any college empowered to teach anatomy, deliver to them the body of purposes of medical or surgical study or dissection."

## *Sources*

### PHOTOGRAPHS

Unless mentioned below, photographs are from author's collection.

Background cover photograph: Gregor Nagele, UM Faculty Portraits, Bentley Historical Library, University of Michigan.

William Herdman, Vertical File, Bentley Historical Library, University of Michigan.

Benjamin Harrison, July 28, 1888. Library of Congress, Prints and Photographs Division, LC-USZ61-480 DLC .

### ARTICLES, BOOKS AND OFFICIAL DOCUMENTS

Ann Arbor City Directories, Various Years

Bierce, Ambrose, *The Devil's Dictionary*, A. and C. Boni, New York, NY 1925

Burress, Marjorie Byrnside, *It Happened 'Round North Bend: A History of Miami Township and It's Borders*, Cincinnati, OH 1970.

Cincinnati City Directories, Various Years

The Cincinnati Times-Star Company, *City of Cincinnati and its resources*, Cincinnati, OH 1891.

Cole, J. A., *Prince of Spies: Henri Le Caron*, Faber and Faber Limited, London, England 1984.

Dickens, Charles, *A Tale of Two Cities*

Edwards, Dr. Linden F., *Body Snatching in Ohio During the Nineteenth Century*, Ohio State Archaeological and Historical Quarterly, Volume 59, Ohio State Archaeological and Historical Society, Columbus, OH October 1950.

Edwards, Dr. Linden F., *The Ohio Anatomy Law of 1881*, Ohio State Archaeological and Historical Quarterly, Volume 46-47, Ohio State Archaeological and Historical Society, Columbus, OH December 1950-February 1951.

Firemen's Protective Association of the Cincinnati Fire Department, *History of the Cincinnati Fire Department*, Cincinnati, OH 1895.

Gibson, William, *Rambles in Europe in 1839*, Lea and Blanchard, Philadelphia, PA 1841

Greve, Charles, *History of Cincinnati*, Cincinnati, OH 1904.

Hamilton County Chapter of Ohio Genealogical Society, *Hamilton County Ohio Burial records Volume 4*, Heritage Books, Cincinnati, OH 1993.

Juettner, Otto, *Daniel Drake and His Followers*, Harvey Publishing Company, Cincinnati, OH 1909.

LaBree, Benjamin, *Notable men of Cincinnati at the beginning of the 20th Century*, George G. Fetter Company, Louisville, KY 1904.

Le Caron, Henri, *Twenty-five Years in the Secret Service: The Recollections of a Spy*, Heinemann, London, 1892.
Roe, George M., *Our Police: A History of the Cincinnati Police Force*, Cincinnati, OH 1890.

Sievers, Harry J., *Benjamin Harrison: Hoosier Statesman, from the Civil War to the White House 1865-1888, Volume 2*, University Publications, New York, NY 1960

*Social Medical Bulletin*, University of Cincinnati, College of Medicine, Cincinnati, OH Various years.

Southey, Robert, *Joan of Arc, Ballads, Lyrics and Minor Poems*, G. Routledge and Sons, London, England (1870?)

Stephenson, Dr. O. W., *Ann Arbor: The First Hundred Years*, Ann Arbor Chamber of Commerce, Ann Arbor, MI 1927.

Warren, Samuel, *Diary of a Late Physician*, Saalfield Publishing Company, Akron, OH 1905

NEWSPAPERS

Ann Arbor Courier, Ann Arbor Register, The Cincinnati Commercial, The Cincinnati Daily Enquirer, Cincinnati Daily Gazette, Cincinnati Daily Star, Cincinnati Daily Times, Cincinnati Journal, The Cincinnati Times-Star, Dayton Daily Democrat, The Evening News (Detroit), Herald (New York), Indianapolis Journal, Ohio State Journal, The Press (Lawrenceburgh), The Register (Lawrenceburgh), The Times (New York), Toledo Blade